His smile teased, but then faded

Leonora lay hypnotized, unable to look away. She forgot her dream as she saw the blue eyes darken almost to black. She ran the tip of her tongue over her lips, heard the sharp hiss of Penry's intake of breath, then his head blotted out the light as his mouth met hers in a kiss that shot a jolt of electricity through every vein in her body.

She tore her mouth away, averting her burning face as Penry got unhurriedly to his feet.

"A mere kiss goodnight," he said softly. "It can't have been your first."

Leonora forced herself to look at him. "I—I don't know. I don't remember." She blinked back tears fiercely. "You may not believe me, but I honestly *don't* remember. Anything."

i

As the soft feminine sound of singing splashed out at him from behind the bathroom door, Amos lay back in bed, squinted out the window at the morning sun, and thought, as dispassionately as he could, about Lila. She wasn't really much of a singer. Oh, she carried a tune the majority of the time, but the sound she made could in no way be considered appetizing. And more than that, of course, was the fact that she was forever forgetting the words.

She had many little habits that drove Amos mad, but none so quickly as when she would butcher a lyric, because not only was he a song writer by trade, but he was a song writer for whom the words were agony while the tunes, at least on good days, seemed almost to leap unbidden from somewhere in his skull. But Lila simply could not remember what rhymed with what. Worse, she didn't care; she just went blithely along. Amos might have spent a day and a half deciding that, though 'crewel,' 'dual' and 'fuel' hardly made an immortal triplet, still that was the best he could manage, but when Lila sang the song, if she ever bothered to, there was no way of predicting what his words would become.

Usually he kept his mouth shut, but the night of their last anniversary had been so horrendous he could suffer in silence no longer.

The evening had been marked for disaster from the start. It was the biggest party they had ever given, eighty-some-odd people. He hated large gatherings, and he knew she knew that; yet he forgave her because he understood she was trying to help him: he had been going through the most ravaging event of his creative life and it had ended in total humiliation, and by luring him into the planning of the monstrous party, he would take his mind off what he had endured. It was their eighth anniversary, and that was the bronze year, and she wondered could he come up with a decorating theme for their apartment that involved bronze and he spent some time pondering before he admitted failure. What about food, Lila wondered; did he have any preferences and he shook his head. None. He had none. Did he mind if she got Jason's to cater? He didn't mind, who was Jason's? Tactfully, Lila explained that they were new but really the very best in town, if you didn't count the cost, but the cost didn't matter all that much, did it? This last was her way of reminding him to look on the bright side, because even though his most recent musical, *Annie's Day*, had just opened to as ruthless a set of notices as any within memory, and even though these notices were nothing compared to what had happened to Amos on the road, still, his previous show, *Francie*, was lucratively alive and about to enter its third smash year on Broadway. So Amos told her fine, use Jason's, by all means.

Then she started on the business with the songs.

During the days she was planning the party, he sat dully through it all, sometimes taking off at noon for a flick, and nothing much got through to him. So when she began pestering him for songs, he was surprised at how spontaneous and powerful his negative reaction was. He hadn't written anything since *Annie's Day* had been in rehearsal and he wasn't about to start now. She retreated, apologizing, but the next afternoon she was at it again, asking for them. He let her have it in the negative and she said 'forget it—

just forget it—' but he knew they were about to enter siege.

'Maybe some parodies,' she'd said that night just before sleep. He didn't bother answering. She went right on, chattering how parodies would fit the occasion better, would save him the problem of actually having to create anything everlasting. All he had to do was just pick a song or two and set some words that fit and she'd never bother him ever with anything again as long as they both should live. Two parodies were all she needed. One about him and one about her. Short. Simple. She kissed him good night as he lay still, her blonde hair flashing for a moment in the November moonlight.

By noon the next day he'd done the damn things.

He awoke with half her song practically done, her name done to the tune of 'Liza, Liza, skies are grey.' For himself, he used 'Once in love with Amy,' substituting his own name in the proper places, throwing in shamus and famous along the way, just to keep his hand in. When he told her they were done she caught him in her arms a while and that was the end of it until halfway through the party itself when the eighty or so people he couldn't have cared less about were ordered into silence by his wife and suddenly in the living-room doorway, there she was, dressed for bed and panicked, Jessica, his own and only beloved, and it came to Amos then that the two terrible parodies were going to be rendered by his six-year-old, who hated large gatherings as much as he did, and Amos realized instantly that Lila had coerced the kid into doing this by telling her that Daddy was going through this bad period and wouldn't Daddy ever be pleased. Amos quick threw a grin on his face and fell to his Steinway, laughing and giving an introductory arpeggio, helping to make sure the kid would be on key, and while she sang, he smiled and laughed, accompanying her as she entertained the people.

The horrible thing was she did entertain them; that was what irritated him more than almost anything. She was a homely little girl, his Jessica was, and growing homelier with the days; at one time, when she was four, she had resembled Edward G. Robinson, but now she was becoming practically a ringer for Bert Lahr. She was the oldest-looking kid in kindergarten by what seemed to Amos at least a decade. But she had the best mind in the family, the best soul on the block, and Amos couldn't think of too many things he was liable to trade her in for.

But seeing her sing and imagining the con job Lila must have whipped up to pressure her into performing was more than he needed right then, so Amos shut his eyes and continued with the accompaniment until the parodies were done. Then as the applause started he opened his eyes and started to open his arms for when the kid would come tearing into them.

Only, Jessica ran to her mother instead. She raced right to Lila, who picked her up, hugging and whirling her around as the clapping sound continued.

And right then, watching his daughter in the clutches of his wife, Amos wanted very much to maim Lila, to kill her slowly, and he didn't want to know all the reasons why.

Now she was darting to him, Jessica, her wrinkled Lahr-like face closing in fast as she said, "Mommy said you'd be surprised, were you surprised?" but she meant only this: 'Did you like it?' Amos knew he could never fake her out, but he gave it all he had with, "Surprised? You better believe I was surprised. And did I ever love it!" They held each other and then she smiled, and probably to most eyes she looked okay, but Amos realized as she left the room that she was only holding back her tears until she found the dark safety of her pillow.

He followed her a casual moment later, leaving the noise of the gathering behind. He opened the wee one's door in silence and there she was, as he knew she would be, pouring out her sad heart alone in the darkness. Amos lingered a moment, and he wondered how he could explain to her that he really did care for her, so much it probably wasn't all that healthy, and who he wasn't so crazy for was not her but their mutual friend, the party giver. But it never would have worked; the kid would have quick claimed all the blame, for she possessed the incredible skill? talent? curse? of rarely believing anything you said about her that was good, especially when it wasn't true, and always believing everything you said about her that was bad, whether it was true or not.

Amos shut the door, returned to the gathering and as a number of guests came around him, complimenting him, he grabbed the nearest drink and guzzled it, wondering what it was he was drowning, wondering what would happen if every time you saw an unattended glass of liquid you drank it; would you die and how long would it take?

From then on, the party got a little fuzzy for Amos. He wandered through the rest of the evening, accepting kisses and anniversary congratulations, and once he overheard two envious ladies estimating the cost of the gathering, which made him smile because so what if *Annie's Day* was a disaster, *Francie* was still alive and the title song was, along with 'Hello, Dolly!' one of the two biggest numbers to come out of Broadway since *Showboat*.

Amos continued drinking, surprised, since he was not a drinker, that he and the rugs were maintaining constant right angles with each other. He did not eat, though the food looked delicious. Lila had decided on two main courses, beef something with a crust, and the chicken that when you cut into it, the spurt of butter ruins your tie.

Though the apartment seemed stuffed with hot and cold running caterers, it was Lila's show. Amos watched her when she was busy doing or talking or moving from one room to another. The face was so stunning. Almost perfect really. A perfect blonde well-bred white Protestant face: teeth any orthodontist would be proud of; pale hair, natural and long; nothing wrong with the skin; or the cheek-bones; or the green eyes. Everything emanated from her eyes; anger, affection, whatever belonged between. And rarely had the green been as glorious as now, because so what if her husband had brought forth a bomb, she was still barely thirty, still totally stunning except for an almost complete lack of chest, which had practically undone her during her teens. She was a thing of beauty and maybe not a joy forever, but right now, she would, by any standard, do.

As the party wore on, Amos wore out, the liquor at last telling, until he realized that there were possibly going to be words spoken after the leave-takings, so he began to stoke himself on coffee. Lila, on the other hand, needed nothing artificial: she seemed to grow more pretty with each flashed smile; each quick conversation made her more fresh, whether it was with guest or caterer. Nothing went wrong. Everyone drank, but no one got surly; everyone ate, but no one spilled. It was just one of those parties, that's all, and what made it happen was Lila.

The last of the visitors remained till well after three. Lila flashed her smile from the penthouse doorway while Amos, standing behind her, contented himself with a drunken wave. He was not remotely drunk any more, but that was a secret, his, and you never knew when it might come in handy. Lila closed the door. "T. G. I. F."

Amos gave her a glance. "Hmm?"

"T. G. I. F." Lila came again. "You know, Thank God It's Friday."

"But today isn't Friday."

"Some of us have been drinking more than others of us," Lila told him, and she turned, heading for the dressing room, unzipping as she went.

"I'm really eluded." Amos followed her.

"T. G. I. F. was what we said at school when the week was over."

"And you're glad the party's over, is that it?"

"He gets there," Lila said. "Not as fast as some, but he arrives."

"You're to be congratulated," Amos got out slowly, "on your triumph."

Lila looked at him. "I thought it went well enough, didn't you?"

They were together in the dressing room now but Amos continued on to the bedroom, where he flopped full length across the bedspread. "I call it a triumph and she asks if it went well enough—I am married to a Wellesley graduate who has reached the age of thirty and has yet to learn that a triumph means an accomplishment, an achievement, at the very least a victory."

"What you say, Amos, and what you mean, Amos, do not always coincide." With that she slipped her dress off, dropped it in the dry-cleaning basket, and moved into the bathroom. He could hear a sink spigot turning on and Lila brushing her teeth.

And then came the sound of her singing.

It was hard for Amos to get all of the slurred syllables, but he could tell it was 'Once in Love with

Amos' she was attempting and any rhymes he had inserted went right out the window.

"Famous," he called.

Lila appeared in the bathroom doorway, toothbrush in hand. "Huh?"

"The rhyme words were famous and shamus," Amos told her.

"That's right," Lila agreed, and she disappeared back into the bathroom.

Amos sat up on the bed. "That's not what you sang," he called.

Lila appeared again in the bathroom doorway, toothbrushless now. "Huh?"

"If you rhymed anything it was 'fame' with 'shame,' which doesn't make sense and doesn't scan."

"Of course it doesn't."

"But you sang them."

"No I didn't."

"Oh," Amos said. "Okay." He lay back down on the bed again.

"Wasn't she just something?" Lila said then. "Jessica."

Amos didn't make an answer. Instead he just stared at Lila, still in her slip, the material barely bulging at all as it traveled down her front from her shoulders. Amos ignored her startlingly pretty face, concentrating instead on her vulnerable body.

"What's the matter?" from Lila.

"Should anything be?"

"You were looking at me funny."

"Oh I don't think so."

"Dammit you were."

"What do you want to fight for?" Amos wondered.

"Who wants to fight, I don't want to fight."

"Oh," Amos said. "Okay."

Lila stepped out of her slip, unhooked her bra, and

for just a moment, before her nightgown covered her, Amos got a glimpse of her boy's breasts.

"Quit staring at my nonexistent boobies, Amos; that doesn't work any more."

"Good night, Lila." Amos managed to yank down the covers and roll in between the sheets.

"With your shoes on. Smart."

"Good night, Lila."

"Those are clean sheets, Amos."

"I'll sleep in my stadium boots if I want to. Now good night. I don't want to fight with you, period."

"All you're doing is fighting."

"Me, uh. All *I'm* doing." Amos threw back the sheets. "Well isn't it odd how a second ago you sang my lyrics wrong and when I called you on it you said I was mistaken—*my* lyrics but you know them better, right?—and I said 'Okay.' Now two minutes later you say I'm looking at you funny and I say not and you just can't let it alone. And *I'm* doing all the fighting."

"They ought to cart you off, Amos; they should really hatch you up before you get dangerous."

"And where'd you get that snazzy idea having the kid perform? I'll betcha Perle Mesta never uncorked a coup like that."

"She was adorable."

Amos stood. "Adorable—if only Gypsy Rose Lee had had you for a mother—"

"—*I will not be crucified!*" Lila moved around the bed toward him. "You're trying to nail me because I forgot your lyrics and I-will-not-have-it!—"

"—you think I give a crap about my lyrics?—"

"—omigod, will you listen to him—if someone changes a semicolon in one of the goddam things the sound of your anguish can be heard in Staten Island—"

"—that may be true, Lila, but not in your case, Lila, because, my pet, the sound of thy sweet voice is enough to make anybody upchuck, and in the second place you remember every syllable Irving Berlin writes and you never goof Cole Porter and doesn't it seem just the least bit ball-snipping that the one composer whose stuff you can't come up with is your husband?"

"He doesn't like my singing," Lila answered. She pressed her hands above her left breast in mock despair. "Break, heart . . ."

Amos lay in bed blinking as the soft feminine sound of singing splashed out at him from behind the bathroom door. The words 'Break, heart . . .' echoed in his head, and there was no question that no one could tick him off like Lila. She was best of breed. Amos stood, wandered to the bathroom, tried turning the knob. The door was locked, so he called, "Hey in there."

"I'm oiling my body, hold your horses."

"You certainly have a gift for phraseology, 'hold your horses.' "

"Remember when you did that thing to me?"

Remembering, Amos said, "No, my sweet, what thing?"

"You counted my clichés. For one entire evening without telling me."

"Ah yes: well that was all in the interests of science."

"Hey out there? Should I put in my diaphragm?"

Amos looked at his watch. It wasn't much past eight. "You don't wanna have some coffee or anything first?"

"You-are-so-unromantic-sometimes-I-could-*scream*."

"Okay, baby, I'll give you a break, what the hell, be a sport, I say." She laughed and he moved slowly back across the room to the windows, looking out at the park. The shadows were still deep, but where the sun touched green, it appeared very strong, hot almost, and several men who moved briskly through the morning carried their top-coats over their arms, as if it were, for all the world, spring.

Amos started darkening the room. He pulled the shades down to below the window-sill level, then began closing the Venetian blinds. When he had that done, he turned off the bed lamps and checked things. There was still some morning light coming in the side of one shade. Amos turned on his bed lamp again, looked around for a towel, and draped it so that it covered the last of the sun, jerking around surprised when from behind the closed bathroom door came her words, "Are you doing that business with the towel again?"

"Just making everything nice and cozy," Amos managed.

"No. It's really very sick Amos. Going to bed with you is like making love in a mine shaft." Another laugh began.

Amos turned out his bed lamp and checked again. The room was dark now. He listened to her laughing, but the sound of it was so full, so genuine, he could only shake his head. "You really break you up, don't you?"

"I liked my mine-shaft line, yes."

"Get out here."

"As you wish, sahib." Then the bathroom door opened, and before she flicked the light out, he got just a glimpse of her good face, her towel-clad body. He could hear her inching forward in the darkness.

"It really is creepy, Amos, having it this black."

He waited, saying nothing, standing by the bed.

"Hum or something so I'll get there faster."

"Waiting here is half the fun."

She found the bed then and slowly worked her way around it. She was a strengthening mixture of glorious odors, oils and perfume and shampoo and talc, and he wished momentarily that he'd shaved, bathed, anything or everything he could think of because he wanted so to please her. Rumpled and pajamaed, he stood very still. In the black he could sense her stopping dead in front of him. Then her fingers. Very lightly at first, roving his body, up to his face, finding his features. Then she lightly kissed him. He still didn't move. He never did. Not yet. Her fingers set to work on his pajamas, unbuttoning the top, spreading the cloth, dropping it back across his shoulders and arms to the floor. Then she found the string to the pajama bottoms, pulled, and he was naked. She moved up body to body with him then, and he could feel the rough wet towel grazing him. "Now you," she said, and at last he moved, his arms only, taking her towel away. As it dropped, her arms went round him and, seeking grace but clumsily, they lowered their bodies to the bed and he was startled, as he always was, at how easily she aroused him. The room was black but he shut his eyes and kissed her at first gently, but then it was too late for that, for her hands were never still and he started to bite her neck until she twisted away in silent protest, spreading, and then at wonderful last, he was inside her, home, there, complete, and he had had more than his share of shafts lately, had tasted it higher than the national average, and this had been the one rock, this moving inside the glorious girl beneath him, and he could feel the pressure building in him but it was too soon, much too soon, so he slowed his rocking down; she understood, suddenly went gentle with him, gentle, almost still, until he felt he could begin to go again, and when he did she understood that too, bucking up from beneath, challenging him, but now in the black he was master of all he could not survey and he relished her challenge, gloried in it until the telephone rang.

"Swell," Amos said.

It rang again.

"Don't answer it please," she whispered.

"Don't worry," Amos said.

A third ring.

"After five they'll get bored," Amos said.

Four.

Five.

Amos held his breath.

Six.

"Christ," Amos said.

Seven.

Eight.

Amos tried moving hopefully inside her.

Nine.

Ten.

Eleven.

She shifted.

He bit his lip.

Twelve.

"How do they know somebody's even here for chrissakes?"

She shook her head.

As he could feel himself starting to go limp, Amos said "sonofabitch."

Thirteen.

Fourteen.

Amos rolled off her, reached toward the sound, grabbed the phone. "Yeah?"

"Why don't you answer sooner; it's like waking the dead."

"Sorry about that," Amos said.

"Are you so hung over in the mornings these days? My God, it must have rung a dozen times."

"Fourteen," Amos said.

"Well?" Lila said.

"I'd like to make this as fast as possible," Amos said.

From the phone Amos heard, "You didn't forget, did you?"

"Forget what?"

"The Lincoln's Birthday party."

Stunned that he had forgotten, Amos said nothing.

"You did forget, didn't you?"

Amos sat up, groped, flicked on his bed lamp.

"I thought you wanted to make this as fast as possible," Lila said.

Amos wrapped his arms tight around his knees. Then, in despair, eyes closed, he began to rock numbly back and forth.

"What's wrong?" Betsy whispered from beside him on the bed.

"Amos?—Amos?—" Lila persisted, her voice metallic over the phone. "You can just answer me."

Softly, Amos managed, "I know what you're trying to do, Lila," and now his voice was louder as he held the phone next to his mouth. "And I'm not going to let you get away with it."

"I really think you're going round the bend, Amos," Lila said, and now her telephone voice was coming in louder too.

"You've just got to try your little zingers, don't you, Lila?" He was almost shouting into the phone now. "I know how it bugs you the way the kid looks forward to being with me and you were just praying I'd forget I was gonna take her to the Lincoln's Birthday party, but no go—" Amos grabbed a copy of *Esquire* from his bed table and shook it at the receiver—"That's my calendar, bitch, and written down for February 12th it says, 'Jessica, kindergarten party'—"

"—quit shouting—"

"—those aren't shouts, baby, those are cries of joy because you must really be panicked about how much the kid cares for me, trying to catch me off guard like this, when you know she's the one thing in the world I give the least crap about—"

The receiver clicked at the other end.

"That's right, hang up, that's a great way to settle things, that's the way losers settle things—"

"—the line is dead, Amos," Betsy said softly from beside him.

"Right, right." He hung up, dropped the *Esquire*, put the phone back on the bed table. He began to rock again, arms around his knees. "How could I have forgotten," he said quietly.

"It happens."

"I shouldn't have forgotten."

"You'll do worse things before you're through."

"Sure, I know that, naturally, but it's a special party, it's just for fathers, a special fathers' kindergarten Lincoln's Birthday party and they make their own invitations and they go to the post office and they mail them and since she's all there is, the kid, it doesn't speak so well of me. I mean, Willie Mays has six hundred homers going into next season; I can remember something gigantically earth-shaking like that, so it can't be senility creeping up. I mean, if she hadn't called—"

"But she did call."

Amos nodded.

"So shape up—it's Wednesday and we agreed on me getting to feel guilty on Wednesdays, remember? I'm Monday-Wednesday-Friday and you're the rest except Sunday we split. Rules are rules, Amos."

Amos reached for her. "You're really very sweet." He kissed her, groped for the bed lamp.

"Not that you're not ravishing, but hadn't you better get a move on?"

Amos looked at his watch. "Right, right." He stood. "I got to pick up the kid; she's probably dressed and waiting." He rummaged around in a large package of laundry, looking for underwear. "Where do you want to have dinner tonight?"

"Maybe we might finesse it."

Her tone made him stop and look at her. She was getting quickly dressed, skirt and bra and shoes, and was searching around for a sweater when he said, "Hey, spiel."

"Nothing to say."

"That dumb I'm not." He crossed to her, took her in his arms.

She shook her head. "I have to go out, Amos."

"What do you mean 'go out'? You got shopping?"

She shook her head again.

"You're taking off?"

In answer, she entered the walk-in closet and grabbed a torn suitcase. Plopping it open on the dresser, she began stuffing it with clothes from the top two drawers.

Amos shrugged, walked over toward the bed. "Gee what a terrific morning. I've had a fight with my ex-wife, forgotten my kid, and my mistress wants to leave me."

"Can't win 'em all."

"Right, right." He got back in bed, pulled the blankets over him.

She went right on packing, but there was too much debris, dresses and books and shoes, and the suitcase could not begin to zip shut.

Amos watched her, remembering how soft and feminine her voice had sounded from behind the bathroom door, and how it had reminded him of Lila's terrible singing, and how did he get from there to here in half an hour?

Betsy hesitated, then tried forcing the zipper, but the case, already torn, began to give. She stopped, her back to him still, staring down at her poor possessions.

"Sweet Betsy Epstein," Amos said then.

She nodded.

"Hey, you're not going to believe this, I know, but last night I got lucky and I hit the sack with this really sweet girl and my God, the way she went on you would have thought she was crazy about me, cared, you know what I mean?"

Her back always to him, she began pressing on her possessions, as if they were some kind of lumpy pillow that could be fluffed into obedience. But the suitcase would not close.

"I'd take that as symbolic if I were you," Amos told her. "Obviously, you're not supposed to go."

"Maybe I could find a shopping bag."

"Fresh out."

"Maybe a big towel then and I'll tie it up like a hobo. Give me a good feeling when I cross the lobby, all those clerks and elevator people watching me." She moved quickly into the bathroom.

"Hey, was that all bullshit last night?" Amos called out after her.

She returned with a towel, dumped some of her suitcase stuff in the center, began tying it up. "Nothing to say."

"Don't you know you're supposed to look your lovers in the eye when you ditch them?—my God, didn't the Girl Scouts teach you anything?"

She turned and stared at him and said, "You know it wasn't, because I've never lied to you and don't make me say things because you're smart, Amos, you can do that, and if I say things I'll come out petty and I'd rather not have you remember me like that."

"'Remember' you? That's a little melodramatic, don't you think?"

Amos could see her control draining.

"Hey, Betsy, easy," he said then, but it wasn't working.

"On the phone," she started, "you were talking to her, Lila, and you said that all you cared about in all the world was your daughter and I understand that, really I do, and I've never made one damn demand on you, but you didn't care remotely for me, Amos, and that's disheartening to a girl."

"That was said in the heat of battle, Betsy."

"That doesn't mean you didn't mean it."

"You can't go over something like that."

"I told you I'd come out petty."

"It's too stupid to even consider—"

"—it's just the latest in a long line of signals, Amos, and if it's so stupid, just tell me something to keep me here."

"It's February, Betsy, and I got divorced in December, so I'm not looking for any permanent entanglements if you don't mind."

"I'm not after permanent—just tell me how much you care for me, Amos—go on."

"I don't want you to leave."

"What's that got to do with caring?—you don't want to be alone, I understand that, I don't like being alone either—anything is better than nothing, like you're all the time saying. Go on."

"I really like your company, Betsy, and that's the truth."

"You can't expect me to turn to jelly over that."

"I'm fond of you."

"Better and better."

"Can I lie?" Amos tried a smile.

She didn't much return it. "No."

"Well I think you're a terrific kid and all that."

She turned back to her packing, making sure the towel wouldn't fall open.

"Hey?" Amos said, and he said it softly, but even as the word came out he could feel the tension behind it and suddenly a scream was loose inside him, an out-of-control scream, and then he was going *"Don't-do-this-to-me-now!"* for the second time in not so many months and as Betsy spun, afraid, Amos fell back, all his blocks crumbling as he was shrouded in *Annie's Day* again and he'd never wanted to do the damn thing from the first, but Donny Klein was his book writer and it was Donny's original idea and Amos let himself be talked into it because Amos hadn't wanted to do *Francie* either, another original of Donny's, and it had made them rich.

So, keeping his lack of enthusiasm to himself, Amos wrote the score, work that never came easy for him but never as painfully as here, because he had so little interest in or respect for the story. It was all about a crazy lady who owned a couple of brownstones in Greenwich Village and she had troubles with wacky tenants and big real-estate interests and several ex-husbands and it all took place in one day, sort of a combination triple steal on Donny's part from *Auntie Mame, My Sister Eileen* and *Madwoman of Chaillot.* There was only one New York run-through and it was a disaster but everybody said so what, all run-throughs were, except Amos knew they all weren't and this show stunk beyond all recognition, which didn't mean he hadn't slaved for it and which didn't make the Philadelphia notices, which were libelous, any easier for him to take. But there was close to a million dollars in the New York advance because the *Francie* team was back in operation, so the first days after the out-of-town opening were about as cheery as possible.

Philly was the only stop, five weeks at the Forrest, and after several meetings it was clear that a couple of new songs weren't going to hurt anything, and if Donny could juice up the book so that anybody cared what happened onstage, that wouldn't be damaging either.

Amos set to work. Slower than normally, because his back was beginning to worry him. He had a thin disc at the base of his spine that every so often kicked up, and Amos was perfectly willing to admit that the problem was mostly psychological, but that never lessened the pain. More and more frequently now, as he sat at the piano, he could feel twinges at the bottom of his spine, and then he would start to perspire, in lunatic fear that he would go into spasm again, become crippled again, which had happened to him more than once in years gone by.

But worse than the problem of the back was the problem of the song. A comedy number was needed, a quintet for Annie and all her ex-husbands who wanted her back, and comedy numbers were always the hardest; even if you were Larry Hart or Porter, you suffered plenty every time you had to come up with a comedy number.

Amos couldn't find a handle right off. He sat in his suite at the Barclay, staring out at lovely Rittenhouse Square, and he couldn't figure out what the hell Annie and her husbands had to sing about that might be both funny and remotely true to character, so after two entire days of stewing, with not one single notion to show for it, he decided to put it out of his head, concentrating instead on a ballad for the stupid male ingenue. Young lovers were always a drag on stage and particularly so here, because the kid playing the part was such a rotten actor. But he was remarkably handsome and had a good voice and with breaks he

was going to make it, most likely in movies. His name
was Dante and he was playing the part of a shy painter
who would never show his stuff to anyone because
what if it was terrible, and Annie gave him in the
second act the confidence to invite a dealer in to look,
and originally that was where his story ended, with
his having the confidence at last to make the move
toward either success or failure.

Only, Donny Klein had decided that it was too
frustrating to an audience, not knowing, so he'd written an additional scene as the dealer exits and after,
when Dante is alone on stage and he sings a song
about, Donny suggested, how he can now love: girls,
beggars, the world, anything. Amos almost upchucked
when Donny first made the suggestion but after con-
siderable discussion, very persuasive on Donny's part,
Amos agreed to give it a whirl.

He got nowhere with that one too. So on the third
afternoon of staring out at lovely Rittenhouse Square,
he called Donny on the phone, said 'Stay,' and elevatored three floors down to Donny's suite.

"So let's hear it," Donny Klein said as he opened
the door. "Move me." Donny was a bouncy little guy
somewhere in his thirties; Amos hadn't the least idea
where precisely, since Donny lied very openly whenever the subject came up. He was unfailingly cheery
and had been a hack TV writer and sometime play-
wright until Amos' music publisher had brought the
two of them together. Their offspring, *Francie,* had
turned into the biggest sleeper since *Bye Bye Birdie*
and they had seen a lot of each other socially since
then. Lila liked him, and although Donny was unmar-
ried, he was never without a stunningly tall girl
named Roberta, who rarely spoke and who Donny
claimed was probably the dumbest girl to ever graduate from Hunter College. Donny and Amos weren't

really intimate—'success friends,' someone had once
called them—but they always got on graciously and
Amos liked the little man about as much as he liked
anybody.

"I'll have to sing it *a cappella*," Amos explained;
"you'll have to imagine the orchestration."

"Go, go," Donny said, and he closed the door, usher-
ing Amos into the living room.

"I've changed the title you wanted; you better know
that before I start, Donny. I mean, it isn't called 'I
Love the World' any more."

"Just do it," Donny said, bouncing a moment before
beginning to circle the couch, something he always
liked to do whenever he heard a new song from Amos.

"You're not mad I didn't use your exact title?"

"*Sing.*"

Amos began improvising. "I love the earth, for all
I'm worth, it gave me birth, outside of Perth, right
near a firth . . ." Amos stopped. "That's just a rough
first draft, y'understand?"

Donny broke up. "You're absolutely *evil*, I believed
you for a second, oh you're foul, Amos, truly not to be
trusted." He continued circling the couch. "Do me the
real one, cur."

Amos sat on the sofa. "Donny, I know it's your idea
to put a new song in for Dante here, and nobody ever
said you weren't smart, but don't you think maybe it's
the least little bit cornball?"

Donny stopped dead. "Are you daring to suggest
that a notion of mine might be stomach-turning?" He
perched momentarily on the side of the sofa. "I'll
admit it runs that risk but look—we're out of town
and we're as they say in trouble, and when you're in
trouble what do you do? You cut every conceivable
bit of dreck and build on your strengths, right?" He
began circling again. "Okay, what are our strengths?

Some great songs by you, some brilliant scenes by me, and a lot of stuff we both should be ashamed of. That we cut. Other strengths? Dante. Believe me. Two movie companies have already sent their talent guys down. I'm telling you, Dante is going to be another Streisand—"

"—he's much cuter," Amos said.

"Haven't you written anything at all, Amos?"

"Nothing I'm satisfied with," Amos said, then quickly, "Hey, what about if instead of a song of triumph it turns out he's a horrible painter—we'd be the first musical in history to have an eleven o'clock suicide song."

"How's the one with Annie and her ex-husbands?"

"You think it's easy whipping up funny showstoppers—"

"—haven't you got anything there either?"

"Oh the idea, sure, I got that. Notes, doodles, possibilities, those I'm loaded with. But I'm still just shy of the final song."

"You'll get it."

"Of course I'll get it!—what the hell do you mean, 'you'll get it'?"

"Don't be mean to me," Donny said. "You know I go to pieces when you're mean." Amos made a smile, turned to go. "*Bubby?*" Donny said then. "You remember out of town with *Francie?* You were worried then too and this one's going to turn out even bigger; it's got to and not because of fate or luck; it's just you're so goddam talented—cut my tongue out, I said it—you are and we both know it, now move your ass upstairs and get inspired."

Amos moved his ass back upstairs, wondering. He knew Donny was just building him up, goosing him along, so that the stuff would come, and God knew Donny had faith in Amos' gifts. Still Amos wondered.

Was he talented? Competent, yeah. Craftsmanlike, no question. But really, no bullshit, talented? Amos just wasn't sure. Oh sometimes he had the confidence— once he'd been walking in Venice back from the ghetto to his hotel and it was late and he was lost and panicked that every shadow was a mugger but on that walk, in that night, he *knew*—gangway Gershwin! —so long Kern!—Mr. Amos McCracken is taking off—

He did not go to the show that night, spending the evening alone in his room, reading a Ross Macdonald. Sometimes he went to the piano, tinkered, then back to the book. He left a wake-up call for seven the next morning, and when it came, he was already up and excited. By eight he had showered, shaved, eaten. By half past he was on his way out for a long walk, because under severe pressure he usually did his best work on the move.

Not even Philadelphia could spoil October. Amos wandered around Rittenhouse Square for a while remembering how Donny said he'd been worried out of town with *Francie* too. And Donny was right—Amos was a worrier but he was damn good on the road— for *Francie* he came up with three new numbers plus additional lyrics for two other tunes, and everything he touched got better.

Amos meandered over to Wanamaker's, took in all the windows, reminded himself he had never seen the Liberty Bell, which was sort of like visiting Agra and skipping the Taj, so he taxied to Independence Hall and looked at it and somehow he'd always imagined it bigger. When it was going on noon, he hit Old Bookbinder's, then strolled along the river until his back began to kick up just the least little, so he taxied back to the Barclay, elevatored to his suite. Then he went to bed and lay very, very still. Because there were no tunes in his head, there were no rhymes on his tongue; beyond 'moon' and 'June' he was helpless.

He had gone, for the first inconceivable time in his life, dry.

There was nothing particularly original about his situation. It was probably sad and certainly true but hardly unique. Broadway was loaded with stories of composers who froze up on the road, who, for no reason, lost it. Amos had even, on good days, fantasied the possibility: what would you do if you went dry, if you couldn't write any more songs? Of course there was never an answer because, always before, if he pushed it hard enough, something inside would begin to shift, adjust, sound.

Not so now.

Amos was amazed at the calmness; no gnashing at all. He was just this sort of lump, this placid, neurotic blob, who happened to be in Philadelphia. He reached for the hotel phone and got the long-distance operator, placed the New York call. The phone buzzed and Lila picked it up. "Long distance for *Jessica?*" she said, confused. "Operator, are you sure—wait—is this a Philadelphia call?" When the affirmative answer came, Lila went "oh ho ho, Amos," and left to fetch their daughter. "It's your funny father," Lila said, and when the kid was on and the operator had given her okay, Amos launched right into "—you have five seconds to guess the tune and win the lollypops—" and began playing 'Shenandoah' on his knee-caps. When she had been smaller, he had always played 'Twinkle, twinkle' but now he had her on folk songs and was planning to start with Rodgers and Hart the year after next.

"It's very hard to tell when you can't see the fingers." She had so few triumphs that when one was presented, she nursed it as long as possible.

"Four seconds."

"Oh I'll never get it, I'll never win those lollypops—"

"—one second," Amos cut in.

"What happened to three and two?"

"Nothing happened to three and two, goofy—they make five just like they always have and I'm terribly sorry but your time is—"

" 'Shenandoah'!"

"Phee-nomenal. Stoo-pen-dee-us. Incredibubble."

"Hi."

"Hi. Why didn't you laugh at my joke?"

"You mean the three and two?"

"At least you knew it was there. I suppose that's something."

"Daddy?"

"What?"

"I'm grreat, are you grreat?"

'Grreat' was her word nowadays, gleaned from *The Flintstones* reruns, all of which she had seen several times, her favorites being the ones leading up to when Pebbles was born, and Amos wondered what in his voice had betrayed him, because she would never have asked if he was grreat if she'd known that he was fine. "Hey, kiss what's-her-name for me."

"You mean Mommy."

"I mean Mommy." Amos made the proper good-byes, hung up, left the bedroom for the living-room piano. He sat stiffly on the bench, noodling chords, changing keys, until the base of his spine exploded and he shrieked, falling against the keyboard, his hands pressing at the wounded area, trying to give it strength, and it must have happened during the phone call, somehow he must have twisted into the wrong position and the pressures of the day had unraveled the spine nerves, and when the nerves went, the disc was left vulnerable and with a sudden desperate move, Amos pushed himself into a standing position. He was perspiring dreadfully now, the pain rising like a heat thermometer along his spine, and he was in genuine spasm, crippled up, or was it one of the temporary attacks that racked him around good but passed on soon thereafter and either way, what he needed was his pain pills but they were in the bathroom medicine closet, miles off, and how was he ever going to survive the crossing?

His left leg was starting to go numb on him as he tried pushing clear of the piano, but the spurt of pain returned him spinning to the instrument, where he closed his eyes, sweat pouring now, and began the trip to his knees and the rug below, careful as any descending climber. He lowered himself as far as he could, then dropped the remaining distance, and the jolt when he landed almost undid him. But he was angry at last, and as he started his crawl toward his medicine he silently cursed his back while aloud, helplessly, he went "anhh-anhh—" with each dreadful slide of his knees. He could not remember any attacks worse than this one—the base of his spine was being ripped away—but he concentrated on that one part of his anatomy, focusing all his madness on the offending disc, until by some miracle, the bathroom was within his grasp.

Amos gripped the porcelain sink, pulled himself up, shifted his weight to one arm and jerked at the medicine cabinet, getting it finally, pulled the pain pills free. It was sweet Thursday, midafternoon, and he needed rest. One pill was usually enough to knock him securely on his ass. Amos took three, crawled to his bed, slept.

Angel was over him.

It was enough to nightmare anybody, that gaunt

face, permanently sunless. 'Angel' Harding had been a successful producer-director on Broadway since after World War II. Amos disliked him greatly, but Angel had been the only one willing to risk doing *Francie*. Immensely tall, dead-pale, he had been a wildly-flagrant homosexual during his years of early success, but now all that was under tight control. "Had the bellman let me in," Angel said.

Amos stirred. It was dark out. "Time?" he said.

"Going on eleven. You keep Scotch?"

Amos nodded. "In the other room." Angel pivoted and was gone. Amos followed him. "I'll call down for ice."

Angel shook his head, Scotch bottle in his hand. "Just a glass'll be fine."

Amos went to the bathroom, took out a clean glass, gave it to Angel.

"Care for some good news?" Angel said, pouring.

"Sure."

"There's a chance I can get Merle Lewis to take a look at the show."

Amos said nothing. Merle Lewis was someone he knew vaguely, a boy-wonder type who had written the big musical of the season past, a rotten show to Amos' mind, but then he was not to be trusted since Merle Lewis' bonanza had replaced *Francie* as the top ticket in town. "Pick his brains you mean?"

"Sure."

"You want to pick his brains, feel free, just don't tell me what he says."

"Fine," Angel said.

The meeting was over but as Amos started to turn back to the bedroom, he realized it hadn't really in fact begun, because Angel would never have awakened him for anything so inconsequential, and before his turn was even half completed, Amos knew a lot of

answers. Still he had to ask the questions, one by one.
"You don't mean 'pick his brains,' do you, Angel?"

"No."

"You want him to stay."

"Yeah."

"And do some writing."

"Yeah."

"In other words, you want his songs, not mine.
You're firing me, that's what you're saying."

"Right."

"Read my contract—you can't fire me." And then
he was having trouble keeping his voice down. "—we
got rich on *Francie*—and now because I'm having a
slow start, I'm fired—"

"*It's Saturday night, Amos!*"

Amos took a step back fast as Angel jumped up,
towering over him, moving in, and for just a moment
Amos contemplated swinging on the bigger man, just
trying to wing one flush on the mouth to see once and
for all if there was any blood beneath that skin, but
his mother a decade dead would have none of it, just
as she never allowed playing catch, climbing trees or
anything else since it would ruin his career as a pianist of great distinction and now she came at him
again with her 'Watch those fingers—careful careful—
mustn't hurt those fingers.'

"Thursday you grab all our sympathy with your
goddam back attack and drug yourself so we can't
expect work but your back didn't hurt you yesterday
and today's gone and where are they?"

"I'll get them," Amos said. "I'm very close to both
of them. That's the truth."

Angel gestured toward the piano.

"I don't want you to hear them till they're completely ready."

"Quit bullshitting me, Amos."

"Let me have just a couple more days."

"I got a six-hundred-thousand-dollar musical dying on me and if Merle's available, I'm gonna grab him."

"Does Donny know you're firing me?"

"Donny's too emotional—I don't need him going to pieces on me—it's best he doesn't know until it's settled and you're gone." Angel drained his glass, filled it. "Your pride's hurt, Amos, I get that, but this isn't good material for you—we need kind of a fantasy touch to pull it off—you'll be fine in a couple of weeks, go get yourself some sunburn."

"I won't let you fire me—I've worked eight months on this turkey, and whatever bombs in New York, I want it to be mine."

"Forget it."

"Donny and me together, we'll fight you—I wouldn't let you fire him—you can't just all of a sudden one night fire me—"

"I just did."

"Dammit I already told you, I-got-a-contract."

"Sure you do—and every show a writer gets fired, he's always got a contract, but just the same, he leaves, because if he doesn't the producer will close the show, that's the standard threat anyway, and the writer can't push it too far because if the producer really does close the show, then the writer's dead because no one will ever invest in anything he writes again, because what if he pulls the same behavior, *capisce?*"

"We got a million advance, you'd never close out of town."

"*I* wouldn't be closing it, *you'd* be forcing me to shut it down—I was trying to fix things, you wouldn't let me, so I did what I had to do rather than embarrass everybody."

"I won't let you fire me," Amos said. "I'll do good work, I promise."

"This happens on half the shows every season—don't let it bug you."

"—You won't be sorry if you lemme stay, Angel—I won't go to sleep till I get something down, I swear—"

Angel drained his glass, moved to the suite door. "Listen, you're all upset, you got a perfect right. But the show's what we have to think of, keep remembering that. I've got a call in to Merle's agent now, and quit making such a beef, all that's happened is I've cut your balls off but they'll grow back if you had any in the first place."

Angel waved, smiled, left.

Amos was about to slam the suite door when he decided against giving Angel the satisfaction, good thinking on his part, and that was what he had to come up with now, he and Donny, a little fancy footwork that would drop Angel to his knees for trying to mess with Amos McCracken. Amos played a couple of dazzling arpeggios on his knee-caps, grabbed the Scotch bottle and, even though he rarely drank, channeled a long swig into his gut which left him gasping, then took the phone. He asked for Donny's suite and when Donny answered, Amos said "stay" and took off down the stairs until he arrived, breathless but ready for battle. Donny took one look at him and said "*Spiel.*"

Amos *spieled.*

Donny blasted off. Amos had never seen the bouncy little man so wild. "That creepy faggot bastard—fire my *bubby?*—we'll fly his ass from Independence Hall." Donny whirled through the room. "Doesn't he know that I, Donald H. for Horowitz Klein can outdevious any sonofabitch around."

For the first time in days, Amos began to feel that everything just might work out after all.

Donny froze, staring at Amos. "You're sure he's making the deal with Merle the pearl's agent right now?"

Amos nodded. "That's what he said—how can we stop it?"

Donny came over and tweaked Amos' cheeks. "Not very bright, my *bubby*. Brilliant with the rhymes, lotsa tunes in there, but dumb." He went to his bar, which was the most elaborate in the company, and poured himself a bourbon.

"Could I have a little Scotch, please?" Amos said.

"My God he's drinking—" Donny poured some Scotch, handed it over. "I'd like to toast my unscrupulous mind—to Donald H. for Horowitz Klein who could have been the greatest agent ever."

"What do we do?" Amos asked, after they drank.

"Getting Angel isn't easy on account of, since he isn't human, you can't appeal to his emotions. But he is the tightest pervert around and that's where we'll get him, we'll kill him in his pocketbook."

"But how do we stop him from making the deal with Merle?"

"We *don't*—we want him to make the deal because that's gonna cost—Merle baby is hot so figure two percent of the gross, if I were his agent I'd get three, but say two. Okay now, they set the deal tonight, and in a while, I go visit Angel, and I manage to get very full emotionally which we both know I can do, right? So Angel naturally thinks I've come to try and save your ass but instead, I say, with the sincerity that only I can muster, 'Have you heard them?' And he says, 'Heard what?' and I say, 'I just visited Amos and he's terribly upset about something, he wouldn't say what, but I got him to play me the new stuff he's been working on and they are both so brilliant I almost cried.' So Angel says, 'Bullshit' and I say, 'They're not fin-

ished, he didn't want to even sing me what he's got,
I had to beg him and he did them and that goddam
kid's a genius!' "

"But I haven't got the songs, Donny."

"Shut up, you've got something done, haven't you—"

"—well, what the hell do you think I've been doing
the last couple days, of course I've got something, but
I can't play for Angel."

"Of course not, dumbo—he fired you, right? He
comes to hear you and you say, 'Sorry, you fired me'
and we'll stall that out long enough for you to finish
the songs. But consider Angel's position: Merle the
pearl's coming down for two percent of the gross a
week, only now Angel-doesn't-want-him-any-more.
He's got you. And when we open big in New York at
a hundred thousand per week gross, the cheapest man
in captivity is going to be paying Merle Lewis *two
thousand dollars a week for not having written any
songs*. Do you know how that's going to gnaw at him?
Do you realize the rearrangement that's gonna cause
in Angel's insides?"

"It would just kill him." Amos finished his Scotch.
"It really would, only what if he decided to use Merle
anyway, since he's got to pay him?"

"No problem—I don't like Merle—wait, that's not
fair—I've never met Merle, it's his work I can't stand
and I ain't agonna work with him. If Angel insists, I'll
walk. With you. We'll both walk. We'll go to the south
of France and live forever." He poured himself another
drink. "Now get upstairs until further developments."

Amos took the stairs to his suite, thought about getting bombed, decided against it, because if Donny
could actually pull this off, and you could never bet
against him on this kind of thing, then sooner or later
he was going to actually have to write the songs.
Somehow. Yes he had this block, but probably Berlin

had them too every once in a while and you had to
work your way through them. Amos went back to his
dead Steinway and played an ugly chord, followed
by one with a little less dissonance, which gave him
at least the semblance of improvement, and softly,
eyes half closed, he pretended he was a cocktail
pianist. Hell, he could always play for a living. Most
of the song writers along the street were mediocre
piano players, some couldn't even play at all; some
played as well as Amos, but nobody any better, and
there was his mother again, going on about his fingers:
'Look, look at them move, you take care of them and
they'll take care of you. . . .'

The knock on the door came a while later, close to
one in the morning, and Amos felt tired as he went
to answer, figuring it had to be Donny, or Angel, or
both. It was neither of them but Amos could not lay
claim to disappointment, since from the very beginning, he had had something of a crush on Tania Snow.
Not that he had ever done anything about it; not that
he ever would; but she was a decent-seeming girl,
extraordinary to look upon, and whenever his wife
was particularly unbearable to him, he would summon
Tania in his mind. He had seen her first a couple of
years ago, when she came in to audition for the second lead in *Francie*. As she walked from the shadows
into the work-light area, Amos could feel his heart,
since she had probably the best body he had ever
seen, topped by a genuinely pretty face. She was
unusually tall, Amos guessed five ten, but round
where it mattered, and an accomplished dancer, as
her audition indicated. She could sing nicely, act
enough, and no one wanted her for the role since she
wasn't what they'd intended. Except Amos. He argued
through the days following her audition, finally winning Donny and Angel over.

Amos knew she would not stay on Broadway long, being too stunning—none of the pretty ones lasted in Manhattan. She was movie material because of the body, Amos was convinced of it, until the first day of rehearsal when she smiled.

It was a terrible smile, and probably she knew it because she smiled so rarely, and then only in brief flashes. It was lopsided and wrinkled her face the wrong way and most of all, of course, it revealed her poor teeth to all the world. Her teeth were large, almost but not quite buck, and terribly irregular. There was no way any orthodontist in captivity was going to make them adequate, and during the rehearsal period, as Amos always surreptitiously eyed her, he saw the pathetic way her right hand instinctively fled to her mouth whenever she was about to laugh. There would be no movie career for this one, Amos realized, no matter how stunning she might be in repose.

She was also, it turned out, something of a gypsy, moving from show to show, getting bored quickly. She possessed none of the stardom drive but even Amos was surprised when she came in to audition for her present part. It was nothing, really, just the girl friend of Dante, the painter who wouldn't show his stuff and whom Amos was going mad trying to write a triumphant eleven o'clock song for. But she auditioned and they grabbed her, as a potential good-luck charm.

"Hey, Tanny," he said as she stood alone in the corridor outside his suite.

"I heard you." She indicated the piano behind him. "So on my way by I knew you were up, feel like company?"

Amos gestured her into the suite. She was the only performer staying at the Barclay, the rest spreading

themselves around three inexpensive hotels clustered
by the theatre. "Drink or anything? Scotch and water
no ice is about the selection."

She looked at him a moment. "Maybe you're a little
tired, Amos, I don't mean to bother— "

"Angel drank out of this earlier," Amos said, indicating the water glass. "I'll try to disinfect it." He
went to the bathroom, turned on the hot spigot and
when the water was close to steaming, he rinsed the
glass, over and over, much longer than need be, for
as the hot thing spun in his fingers it brought back
Angel and Amos understood that at least in part
Angel had lied: he would never have fired one song
writer without having another already on ice somewhere, so all the business about trying to make a deal
with Merle the pearl's agent had to be bull.

He dried the glass, a little confused, wondering
what his realization changed, if anything. Back in the
living room, Tania was standing by the window. She
was wearing a pale-blue sweater that went well with
her eyes and as Amos poured her drink he said,
"You'll have to forgive me, but I'm particularly paranoid tonight."

"How so?"

Amos gave her the glass, took a swig from the
bottle. "Like since you don't stay on this floor, and
even if you did you wouldn't pass this room on your
way from the elevator, I just wonder how you so
casually came knocking at one in the morning?"

"Trapped." She sipped her Scotch. "It's just that
some kids in the show knew we were friends from
Francie and were after me to ask you about things.
There's a lot of wild rumors, Amos."

Amos waited.

"Like is the show gonna close? That's what everybody's trying to find out."

"Angel has a million advance in New York, he's not about to close. A million ensures at least four, five months, even with bad notices. You know how much Angel can steal in that time? Swiss banks have been known to start on less."

Her smile flashed briefly but painfully, her right hand making its instinctive move. Then she was in repose again and Amos thought her one of the great sights; flawed, but when viewed under the proper conditions, startling. She took a long swallow on her drink.

"Any other rumors?" Amos wondered.

She looked at him. "Should there be?"

Amos shrugged.

She finished her drink, put the glass down by the piano.

It crossed Amos' mind to offer her a refill, and he could feel himself starting to flush because for a minute, they were almost on a boy-girl plane, somewhere they'd never been, only friends, sexless, even though he had always found her more than desirable and had never slept with a dancer and everyone always said they could do fantastic things with their bodies. But he had enough on his mind right then, and besides, he had not once since their wedding day been unfaithful to Lila, even though he wasn't sure sometimes if that was bragging or complaining.

"Care for another?" Amos asked as she started to cross the living room.

She looked at him again. "You sure you want me to, Amos?"

Amos wondered what she would do if he made a pass at her. Jesus, who was the last girl before Lila he'd made a pass at? She was probably a grandmother by now. "Why not?" He filled her glass fuller than the last time. He could always fake making a pass, just maybe accidentally graze one of her magnificent boobies while he was handing her the drink, and if she didn't object, then—

What if they weren't hers? Lots of dancers wore falsies. So maybe he grazed her and she didn't make a fuss and the next thing he'd get her sweater off, unhook her bra, lift it up and what if there wasn't any breast there at all, what if she was built like Lila, flat, with just a couple of big nipples tacked on to break the monotony? Who needs it, Amos decided. I got troubles of my own. "Hey, Tanny—do me a favor? No big deal or anything, but you know a guy named Merle Lewis?"

"Course. I auditioned for his show last year."

"Well, see, it wouldn't be inconceivable for him to show up in Philly sometime, and if that happened, and you saw him, if you'd let me know, I'd appreciate it."

"He's here, Amos."

Amos nodded, not really all that surprised. "You've seen him yourself?"

"Course."

"Recently?"

"This afternoon at the matinee."

Amos almost smiled, because he was really zeroing in on Angel—bring Merle down, get him to take the job, make sure everything was all done and pat before paying his visit.

"He watched most of it with Donny Klein," Tania said.

Amos shook his head quite violently. "I think you're a little wrong there, Tanny."

"Amos, I'm really not."

"You've got things a little twisted there Tanny is what I'm telling you," Amos went on, louder.

"Okay, Amos."

"I mean, Donny's devious, but he's not that devious. I ought to know, don't you think?"

"Course."

"I suppose you're going to tell me you saw them yourself and you couldn't be mistaken."

"It was just gossip," Tania said.

"Then you didn't actually see them."

"No."

"It's all just rumor."

"Yes."

"Are you lying to me now?"

"Course."

"I knew it." Amos managed. "I knew you were. I just . . ." And he shook his head wearily. "Aw, shit . . ." He found his way to a chair.

"That's what everyone was saying, Amos—that you'd been canned. That's why I came up, to find out. I was thinking of quitting the damn show anyway."

"Why?"

"It's no good once they start the crapping around firing people. They probably would have cut my part out, or at least down, Donny's so sure Dante's gonna be a great star."

Amos heard the phone. He got out of the chair and moved into the bedroom, closing the door in the darkness. Then, groping toward the sound, he took the receiver and lay flat in bed, eyes closed tight.

"It was beautiful," Donny said. "You've never seen Angel so shook."

Amos didn't know what to say so he simply made a sound as Donny hurried on.

"Well there's no chance of Merle working on the show—no chance at all. I mean, after the sell job I did on your new numbers—Angel's trying to stop his coming down and get out of the deal but there's less chance of that happening than Hoover turning straight so—"

"How was the matinee?" Amos said then.

There was a pause. "Performance was a little down I thought," Donny said; "the usual 'Saturday they're working me too hard' blues."

"How was the matinee?" Amos asked again.

"You potted?—didn't you hear what I just—"

"Don't do this to me now!" Amos screamed.

Donny came right back with "How'd you find out?"

"I never would have fucked you like this, Donny—"

"We don't know that, Amos."

"Never, I swear."

"I've worked too long on this show to wash it down the drain—if you'd written the new songs none of this would have happened—if you're looking for someone to blame, blame yourself, Amos, and kindly include me out." Donny hung up.

Whipped, Amos just lay there a while, holding tight to the dead receiver. Eventually, that seemed fruitless, so he fumbled around, put it back in its cradle, thinking now only of vengeance: Angel and Donny, how could he bring them down, and of course he would have to forget Donny's words, 'if you're looking for someone to blame, blame yourself, Amos,' 'cause if he remembered them for too long, and if he stayed tuneless, all his pretty rage would spill on his own psyche since he was just masochistic enough to think, at some date in the not too great distance, 'they were right to fire me, I'm not saying they went about it in exactly the most honorable way, but all in all, they were right, they were, I have to admit it, not that it didn't bother me at the time, but now, recollecting in tranquillity, I can honestly and truly say that even though it killed me, God was on their side.'

The bedroom door opened. "Amos?"

"Tanny?" He lay as before, not remotely moving. "I forgot about you." Then, "That's pretty flattering, wouldn't you say?"

"They fired you, huh?"

"They fired me, huh."

"Fuck 'em."

"Oh yes."

She sat down on the edge of the bed and he moved over to give her a bit more room and in the darkness as he moved his arm grazed some part of her, he wasn't exactly sure which, but whatever it was it was not as covered as usual. "*Jesus, Tanny, where are your clothes?*"

"In the living room."

"I don't mean geographically, I mean psychologically, what the hell are you doing?"

"You've just got to be in analysis."

"No, I'm not in analysis it so happens, I was, but I quit, no, not quit exactly, I was finished with anyway, I don't mean I was discharged or anything, it just wasn't doing me any good and Lila—that's my *wife*, Tanny—she felt bad I was in and since it wasn't doing me any good and we had this big reconciliation in Europe summer before last, so when we came back I didn't go any more." He was on the far edge of the bed now. "My analysis isn't important, Tanny—I'm a married man and next month we celebrate our eighth wedding anniversary and I've never been unfaithful yet and I was never tardy in grammar school either."

"Grammar school? Easy, Amos."

"It's easy for you to say 'easy' but what if Lila walked in now?—me caught in bed with a dancer."

"You're dressed."

"You think the goddam *New York Daily News* would mention that? They know what sells, the sonsabitches."

"I didn't mean to unhinge you, Amos."

"I'm not unhinged, for chrissakes, but wouldn't you be unhinged if you were taking a little snooze and some guy walked in bare-assed naked? I mean, the most intimate thing I ever did to you was buy you an egg salad sandwich after rehearsals and I'm still waiting for an explanation."

"I turned off the living-room lights and I got undressed and I came in here. It's very late and I never sleep with clothes on."

"That sounds logical, except for one thing: you've got your own room, am I right? Huh? Huh?"

"God, Amos, it's just that if I'd gotten fired on the road in the middle of the night I wouldn't want to be alone, that's all."

"I don't want to be alone," Amos said.

"Well then shut up all this inquisition business and let's go to sleep."

"You go to sleep. I don't feel like getting undressed just now. I just wanna lie here and think."

"There's no way I can rape you, Amos."

"It's not that, who's worried about that, but you're not a dog, Tanny, and I've got the good conduct medal eight years running now and you're not worth losing all that for—there I go flattering you again—" Amos lay on his side of the bed while she got in the other and pulled the covers over her.

"They fired me off *Fair Lady*," Tanny said then.

"You're not that old."

"Not the original company—this was the dregs, a chorus part in a summer stock package. It was my first job, big break in the business, all that. They got rid of me when we were playing Beloit, Wisconsin. That was what I couldn't get over—if they'd done it in Chicago, well, Chicago's a big city, but when you bomb in Beloit, friend, that's bombing."

"What'd they fire you for?"

"They said I was too tall, I stood out too much, and I remember bawling at them, 'Then why'd you hire me?—I haven't *grown*.' What'd they fire you for?"

"They didn't like the new songs I wrote."

"What the hell do they know? Donny's a book writer and Angel I've been directed by twice now and he's got a tin ear, lemme tell you. After all you did for them on *Francie*—"

"—they were right to fire me—there weren't any new songs—I lied to them just like I lied to you only they didn't swallow it—there weren't any new words, no tunes, no goddam thing at all, I'm dry," and in the midst of his outburst he could feel her shifting toward him across the bed and as her arms took him he almost said 'I don't want your pity' and the only reason he didn't actually verbalize the thought was because by that time she was on him, her tongue in his mouth and he realized it wasn't pity she was selling, and as their bodies locked with the blankets between them Amos could tell resisting her was going to be difficult, not impossible but not easy either, and then, while the kiss lingered, she fought the sheets and blankets down and Amos, almost in fear, reached his hands down toward her breasts and when his hands found them he decided he must never let go, for it had been eight years since he had fondled anything splendid there, anything other than nipple over bone. He stroked her and fondled her and in the darkness she was fumbling with his clothes and doing as well as could be expected but it wasn't fast enough for Amos, not nearly, so reluctantly releasing her he ripped at his clothing while she kissed him and when he at last was naked they plunged down onto the mattress, and he understood about being gentle but that was with Lila while this one by virtue of her curves just ruled it out of the question and Amos kissed her a few more times before mounting her and, throbbing, with the timing that could only come from God, managed to separate her legs, and then, just before he began the ecstatic moment of actual penetration, came.

Things got very quiet in the room.

"Maybe I better get a towel, Amos."

"Sometimes I last even longer."

"It's okay, really, but I think maybe you better get off me while I get a towel—we're soaking the sheets."

"I'm surprised you can even move after going through an orgy like that—Christ, Tanny, how does it feel being debauched by the old master?" Limp and discomfited, he rolled off her and sat on the edge of the bed while she hurried to the bathroom. "Sex is really something when it works, wouldn't you agree? Tell the truth now, anybody ever flood your navel with that kind of finesse before?"

"Like they say, accidents happen."

"You call it an accident? That's like calling Krakatoa a mishap. Eight years and I didn't even get inside you, Tanny."

"I was there, Amos, and that's certainly true."

He got up then, hit the living room, flicked the lights on and off to get a reading on the Scotch bottle. Naked in the darkness, he grabbed it by the neck and sank to one end of the couch. He took a swallow, grimaced, took another, felt his stomach rebelling, overruled it by taking a third.

"Amos?"

"I'm here, Tanny, but if you don't mind, I'd like a litle private penitence."

"That's what I wanted to tell you." She made her way to the couch, sat at the far end from him. "Look —you got nothing to feel bad about, because you didn't do anything."

"I'm sure you're representing a good cause—"

"—figure it this way: if I'd been a virgin, I'd be a virgin, so what did you really do? Nothing."

"Don't you understand?—*that's* what I feel so guilty about—I mean, if I'd at least lasted, I'd have some flashback material."

"Scotch?" she asked. He stretched his arm across the sofa. Their hands met, she took a sip, handed the bottle back.

Amos took another small swallow. "I've got nothing, Tanny—ashes I have. In my mind I'm guilty for doing something and in my body I'm guilty for not doing something. Keep your eyes on the referee, 'cause someone's killing me."

"Well I just think you shouldn't feel so guilty."

"Not feel guilty?—I'm a Jew—it's what I do best."

"Swig?" She reached for the bottle. "That's a wild Jewish name, McCracken."

"Half I am." He shook his head. "God, the way the important things in your world change on you. That was my big secret in college—no one knew. And when I came to New York, no one knew. My folks are dead, I got one aunt somewhere in the Pacific Southwest—who's gonna guess? And a year and a half ago, when my marriage was in kind of trouble and we went to Europe, in this great revelation, I let Lila know my mother was a Jew—Lila was in the dark too—and it was this incredible unbelievable stone off my insides, the secret was out." Amos shrugged. "Now I tell elevator men."

"I'm all."

Amos looked at her in the darkness. "Jewish?"

"Course."

"Lemme," Amos said, and she handed him the bottle. "The name isn't."

"My God, you don't think anybody actually calls

their kid 'Tania'? Not in Oberlin, Ohio they don't. I picked it. Originally I was 'Tanaquil' because I saw LeClercq dance once and she was my idol. Then when it turned out I wasn't going to make much of a prima ballerina, I had to switch—I didn't want to sully her, but by then everybody was calling me 'Tanny' so I took Tania, it was closest. The 'Snow' was for, I don't know, being born in December maybe or maybe I just thought it sounded classy, but I'm born Betsy Epstein." She stood then and started across the room, away from the couch toward the window.

"That's not such a terrible name," Amos said as she went.

"I didn't think it would go too great on movie marquees."

As she approached the window she became vaguely visible—on the couch she had been only sound—and as the night hit her naked body, Amos was impressed again with both the size and shape of the package. She leaned against the windowpanes, staring out. "You're really kind of a great looking girl," Amos told her.

She shrugged. "Except when I smile."

"What's wrong with your smile? — it's a terrific smile."

"Oh Amos, don't bullshit me—I have been haunted by that stinking smile since I can't remember."

"Right, right," Amos muttered. "Let's say it's not your greatest feature and leave it at that and hey?— I never bullshit, really I'm practically compulsively honest a lot of the time, so forgive me for then because I'm not myself right now on account of you can't imagine how guilty I feel."

She whirled at the window. "That same tune—it's disheartening to a girl. Amos—search your soul and tell me—burrow in there—root it out—*how goddam guilty do you feel?*"

As he sat concentrating on the creature by the window, the answer was immediately apparent: he didn't feel so guilty. "Hey, Tanny, you wanna try again?"

"In other words, what you're saying is that all this shame and remorse have just been more bullshit."

"Why don't we put it that I find I can handle the emotion a little easier than I maybe thought—how 'bout the sack?"

"Well I like you and all, Amos, but how do I know you're not going to start with how guilty you feel that you don't feel guilty?"

"I can't promise."

"Then no deal."

"You got nothing to lose—what can happen? I can't do worse."

"Sure you can—look on the bright side: there's always impotence."

Amos had to smile. "You were really something by that window."

Betsy went on packing. "What window?"

"Back in Philly. The night they fired me."

"I was younger then." She tied the towel as securely as she could, managed at last to zip her suitcase shut. Then she took a breath, staring at her wrist, at the beautiful bracelet of antique gold. It had been a gift from Amos and was the only inanimate thing she seemed to care for. Now she turned it slowly around her wrist, watching it closely. "I don't really want to go, Amos. But I'm twenty-seven and you're a fiend, and that's just not a winning combination."

"Hey Betsy?"

She picked up her tacky suitcase, grabbed her knotted towel.

"I lost my wife my eighth anniversary when we started with a little bicker over her not being able to remember my lyrics—they were the first words I'd written since I'd gone dry in Philly so they were kind of important to me, but still not the kind of thing you lose a wife over, but I did. Don't let me lose you over a kindergarten party."

"Oh Amos, if only you had."

He watched her go. No more Sweet Betsy Epstein. Amos lay in bed, contemplating the size of his loss: she wasn't all that bright really, and, of course, she was a dancer which automatically meant she was crazy. Other than that, though, and forgetting her smile, there wasn't too much major wrong. She was as good a lady as was ever going to be able to put up with him.

And even if she'd been worthless, she was company. He'd taken his present room, despite the fact that it was in a residential hotel full of dying biddies, because it was closest to the old apartment, which made it easy to skip on over and go meandering with the wee one. Lila, whatever her faults, was perfection when it came to visiting: no strings, period. Just call and if it worked with everybody's schedule, as it usually did, swing. So he'd taken this room. It was small, and he kept it clean but messy, since if he ever took to tidying up, that could mean he was possibly planning to live there. Chilling as that might be, colder was the coming in each night knowing that everything was precisely and exactly as he had left it, hours before. That was why Betsy was so precious; at least she warmed the place, kept the air in circulation while he was out getting the papers.

But now he was alone, again, and already he could feel it, so he hopped into the can, shaved and showered, beautified his body, dressed. He had to go over fast, pick up the kid for the party, so he decided on a Chipp dark-grey suit, very conservative, making sure none of the other daddies could look down on him as some goddam bum of an artist. White button-down shirt, red knit Saks tie adding a dash of pzazz, black support socks to give his back a little edge, cordovan Florsheims and a lined Aquascutum trench coat for that final fillip of mystery.

Resplendent, he got the hell out and was almost at the elevator when he remembered his mustache.

He pushed the buzzer twice, then beat it back, unlocked the door, found the mustache on the desk top. Running now, Amos closed the door on the fly, got to the elevator just before it came, carefully put the mustache in his suitcoat pocket as the door opened. Terry was on. Terry was old and Irish, and when he'd first moved in, Amos had given him a free pair to *Francie* because it never hurt to have friends, only it turned out old Terry loathed the show and told Amos about it incessantly for weeks afterward. Now Terry made a slight nod.

Amos made one back, thinking 'fuck 'em all' as the doors slid shut behind him.

ii

Amos was surprised by the morning. The feel was more May than the middle of February; the sun was really very strong, amost cleansing, and there was no wind. He grabbed an empty cab—the day's first decent symbol—and gave the East End address. Ordinarily he would have walked the blocks from Madison, but his kid was just as antsy as he was about time, and he had probably kept her waiting already.

He sat back, taking the bumps as they came, and wondered if Lila was going to give him lip for any particular omission. God, the way they fought. More almost since the split-up than before, which surprised him. If she's gonna give me trouble, Amos decided, I better be in battle condition, so he said casually to the Caucasian in the front seat, "Thank God for Lindsay."

The man rose magnificently to the bait, jerking his head around. "Howzat?"

"Mayor Lindsay," Amos explained patiently. "The things he's done for the city. Marvelous."

"He's a fuckinniggerlovinprick."

Amos tried for astonishment. "You don't like John Lindsay?"

"What are you, some outta-towner? Between what he gives the colored and what he gives the Spanish, he's turned this town into a shit heap." The man gunned the car past Lex and had a decent shot at making the light on Third.

"It's a free country," Amos said, "and you're more than welcome to your opinion." He sat quietly a moment before driving the stake into the heart. "But clearly, you don't know the city."

The man began to redden. "I don't know the city— *I* don't know the city—I only been pushin' a fuckin-hack thirty years in this fuckintown and you're tellin' me *I don't know the city*—"

Amos relaxed happily in the back seat as the discourse from the front built in volume. When they got to the East End building, Amos tipped the man, thanked him for the entertainment and walked in past the doorman.

"Hot enough for you, Mr. McCracken?"

"Beautiful, huh Charley," Amos answered, heading for the front automatic elevator. It was waiting, so he stepped in, pressed PH, started on his journey. It was really a pretty decent building, even though it wasn't old. They'd taken it right after *Francie* hit, and when the pfffft came, Lila decided it would be best for her to stay put, easier on the kid considering all the other changes that would be going on around her. The apartment rented for a ton, but Amos agreed, since he could afford it easy enough as long as his royalties held, and the place was big and had a great view of Carl Schurz Park and the East River and the kid loved looking at the boats.

There were only two penthouse apartments and Amos veered left, pausing only briefly by the door, debating his entrance. He diddled rhythms with the doorbell, letting the kid guess his presence and his mood. If the dumps had him he'd hit the 'yo-ho-heave-ho' part of the 'Volga Boatman' and if he was particularly manic he'd ring the start of 'Zip-a-dee-doo-dah' which drove Lila straight up the walls, but now he concluded he was at his pzazziest, so he did the corn-ball 'shave-and-a-haircut-two-bits' routine on the doorbell and waited. Usually from inside he could catch the kid's footsteps but now there was nothing, which meant probably she was busying herself on the potty, so he did it again, 'shave and a haircut, two bits,' and was about to begin a third go-round when Lila flung the door wide open, already into anger: *"Christ —can't you do anything right?"*

Amos counterpunched instinctively, dropping fast to one knee. "But soft, what light through yonder window—"

"What in the name of God are you doing here, Amos?" She glared down at him, her hands very firmly on her hips.

Amos stood. "That's a fairly cretinish question, considering you woke me up around an hour ago with orders to get my ass in gear."

"The party's at the school, beanbag—"

"—you sure?—"

"—Amos you were sent an invitation—Jessica made it herself and mailed it herself and it very clearly stated you were invited for the party at the school for ten-thirty to twelve on Lincoln's Birthday."

Amos glanced at his watch, saw that it was still shy of ten.

"I marvel you can get through the day at all, Amos —you haven't done anything right since New York was a colony—"

"—score one for you—" He wet his index finger with his tongue, made an imaginary mark in the air.

"—it's not funny, Amos, it's bloody irritating is what it is." She was wearing her nightgown and her hair was mussed and she would not take the anger from her eyes.

"Hey, it's not that big a deal and if you're absolutely sure you mean that coffee invitation, I accept."

"I'm not offering you—"

"—just a cuppa will do me—I mean it—I haven't

had any this morning and my entire future may depend on—"

"—Amos you've got a party to go to, good-bye—" She started to close the door.

He slipped quickly inside. "I can walk to the school in two minutes, Lila, that's why we wanted her to go there, remember? Now please, I'm early. I'll take instant."

"You can damn well buy your own coffee outside—"

"—Amos—" "sweet? Butter wouldn't melt in your month—"

"—at least do this for me." He took the mustache from his pocket, held it out to her. He had planned on having Betsy handle the repairs, but that wasn't possible now, so Lila had to be the one to do the needlework, even though she would never make Coco Chanel worry. "See?" He pointed to the mustache. "Right where the thing clips on my nose, it's starting to fray —just sew it tight around for me, huh? And use black thread to match the color if you've got it."

"I'm not going to fix your stupid mustache! Now get out of here."

Amos, genuinely surprised by her rejection, tried one more time. "The whole thing can't take you more than two seconds, Lila."

"I'm gonna start screaming in a minute, Amos—"

Amos looked at her, closely this time, and he knew this creature *muy* well, thank you, so it only was a moment before he decided that what he had taken for anger in her green eyes was something much closer to panic. "Hey—"

"Amos, do you want me to ring for the doorman? Is that what you passionately crave, to be thrown out so that the news sweeps the building?"

"Hey, is everything okay with you, Lila? Really now."

"No, everything is not okay with me really now—

I'm standing cheek to jowl with you—how in the
world could everything be okay with me really now
when you're in the vicinity?"

"Lemme be sure I understand all this, Lila—are
you trying to tell me you want to try a reconciliation?"

"I can't stand it when you start cracking wise—
just go, huh—it's not my day, and I'm late, Amos, I'm
doing some charity work and Jessica couldn't make
up her mind what she wanted to wear to the stupid
kindergarten party because it had to be perfect for
her damn daddy and that got me further behind and
there are some very important women arriving here
for a very important meeting to discuss fund raising
and I'm running so late I want to just cry and that's
all, Amos, now shoo."

"I think you're lying to me," Amos said. "I do not
remotely believe you."

"I don't care what you believe, Amos—*move your
ass!*"

Amos hesitated a moment.

"Don't you know why our marriage didn't work—
it's moments like these—Jesus, living with you is like
having shingles—no woman can live with you—they
go mad!"

Staring at his onetime wife, who had left him,
thinking momentarily of Sweet Betsy, who had acted
not dissimilarly, Amos thought that maybe she was
right this once, Lila; maybe the cesspool he seemed to
be living in lately was his own doing, not the whim
of an unjust God after all. So, trying very hard not to
show just how punishing her latest blitz had been,
Amos was totally prepared to depart when the cavalry
came, for, from deep in the heart of the apartment,
clearly in the direction of the master bedroom,
sounded a deep masculine voice calling, "Everything
all right out there, Lila?"

In the February morning, Amos stretched. "Fella come to fix the air conditioner?" he inquired idly.

Lila threw her hands around her body in wild frustration and turned to the nearest available wall.

"Hey, Lile?" the masculine voice went, closer this time.

"The iceman cometh," Amos said.

Lila didn't say much.

Then a third force entered the foyer, stopped. Quietly, Amos eyed his successor. The guy was standing there, big and barefooted, wearing dark-grey slacks and a white button-down shirt that was hanging out in the back. His hair was mussed. He was as dark as Amos had been fair, as thick as Amos was slender. Without shoes, he was probably an inch over six, while Amos was an inch under with. Surprisingly, his face was delicate, the features fine. His bloodlines were probably, like Lila's, all any WASP's should be.

Lila turned back into the room, saying lightly, "All right, I fibbed, big deal, it wasn't charity."

Amos smiled, "Having been in bed with you myself, over a number of years, let me assure you that charity is all it could be."

"Watch it," the dark-haired guy said.

"Oh Freddy, Jesus," Lila said, "that's just Amos cracking wise, you don't even hear it after a while."

"I just don't like people talking like that when I'm around," Freddy said.

"Freddy, Amos isn't people—he's just this object that gets washed up by the tide every so often."

"I want him out of my apartment," Amos said.

"It isn't your apartment," Lila said.

"It's Pease and Elliman's if you want to get technical but I pay the rent and he's not in the sublet clause."

Freddy pointed to the front door. "Bye," he said to Amos.

"Who *is* he?" Amos demanded.

Lila did the introduction. "Freddy Hunter, this is clearly Amos."

"Freddy Hunter?" Amos said. "Frederick A. Hunter? *The* Frederick A. Hunter?" He shook his head. "You don't know the things I've heard about you—back when we were courting—my God, the bilge Lila fed me about Frederick A. Hunter whose daddy was the capital B Banker—you were my chief competition all those years ago and what I want to know is how could you have been such a bastard as to let me win? They shouldn't have killed Eichmann, they should have let him live with Lila for a while."

Lila smiled. "I don't even hear it any more, Amos. Were you saying something?"

Freddy took a step toward him. "You smart-ass bastard."

For just a moment Amos contemplated tangling with the bigger man, knowing he'd lose but maybe he'd get in one good one before he took his battering, except his mother wouldn't let him, not under any conditions as angrily Amos heard 'Those fingers are your fortune, are you crazy?—those are all you've got, and they're worth gold' and Amos nodded, again the loser, extending his own world record until as he reached the door everything fell together into one question and he whirled on Lila loud asking, *"Did he spend the night?"*

"—no—of course he didn't—"

"How come he isn't shaved then?—how come a big-deal banker's son walks around East End Avenue unshaven Wednesday mornings?"

Lila looked at Freddy. She shrugged. "I don't know. Why didn't you shave, Freddy?"

"You don't have to answer him, Lile—he's not your boss any more—"

Amos moved a step toward her. "How could you let him?—you know what that must do to the kid?—"

"*I didn't let him, Amos!*"

"You've always lied rotten—all the apcray you were giving me before, about how the kid couldn't decide what to wear because she was so anxious to please her daddy—that was supposed to knock me out with joy so I wouldn't wonder why a mother would get all dressed to take her kid to school and then get back in a nightgown when she has this big charity meeting about to happen—Jesus, Lila—"

"—Jessica never knew—"

"—that's right—" from Freddy.

"Well that's different then," Amos said.

"We came in late," Lila explained. "She was already asleep and I paid the sitter and we snuck into the bedroom and locked it and this morning I didn't let her go back."

"I see," Amos said. "You bring goddam King Kong home to hit the sack with you and the kid, being obtuse, as we both know she's always been, doesn't catch on—I mean, the fact that her sweet mommy bars her from her bedroom which she's never done before wouldn't raise her suspicions—and naturally the fact that she wakes up all the time in the middle of the night wouldn't happen with him here and if it did, she wouldn't come see you."

"Amos, on my word of honor—"

"Easy, Lila," Amos said. "There's no point in getting passionate and pledging your life away. You say you were alone you were alone, fine. I'll just ask the kid and I'm sure she'll corroborate everything."

"You better not do that, Amos" Lila said.

Freddy looked at Lila. "He's got us, what's the big deal? We didn't do anything wrong and I'm not ashamed of a damn thing. And little Jess is just fine."

"How many other guys have spent the night here?" Amos asked. "I mean, is it like one of those poverty cases you're always reading about where every night there's a different 'uncle' sharing the sack with moms?"

"Nobody else. And last night was the first time."

"I'm sure the kid will corroborate that too," Amos said.

"Oh I'll get you for this Amos," Lila began. "I swear to God, I swear to God—" and she turned away.

"You just love upsetting Lile—"

"The knife cuts both ways," Amos answered.

The bigger man started advancing on him then, voice tense and down. "You listen to me, you prick bastard, you're done upsetting this family and if you want to know what's going on, this is the first time in her life little Jess has gotten anything worth shit from a man—"

"Meaning I don't care for her, right?" Amos said. "I don't now and I never did and—"

"—meaning just what I said, no less and no more, you're so fucking smart so you claim, figure it yourself on your way out," and he was up next to Amos now bulling him back toward the door and Amos turned like a good boy, catching a glance of Lila as he made his move but not long enough to tell whether it was scorn for him showing in her green eyes or triumph for herself, maybe a little of each with plenty of gravy and his hands were clenched but there was his mother with her admonitions, 'oh, don't you dare, it would ruin everything, *everything*,' her voice growing louder and louder till Amos topped it with one giant "*Shut up!*" and as he shouted he whirled back on his tormentor, throwing a sudden awkward punch at the unshaven face, and naturally it missed, hitting only air, but Amos had another ready, a right this time, and as

he threw it he only prayed that before he was humiliated completely one of his punches would land, just
one, preferably somewhere soft, like on the lip or the
cheek or even the side of the nose but his right went
wild too, landing forceless on Freddy's shoulder and
as Freddy stepped back, bellowing, Amos thought oh
Jesus, he's gonna kill me, so he ducked into a protec-
tive crouch trying not to listen as Freddy continued
bellowing at him, circling, ready to cripple him quickly and Amos wondered how badly it would hurt and
could he back out now but the answer was a fast no,
not and be able to face even a cracked mirror, so he
left his crouch and threw a roundhouse right and
thank you Sweet Jesus, it landed, it *landed,* right on
Freddy's lip as if divinely aimed and the force of it
surprised Amos because it hurt his hand, hurt it like
hell, and his mother was on him now, crying and be-
seeching him to stop but Freddy's lip was bleeding
just a little and Amos realized it was true, all the crap
he'd read about what happened to you once you
tasted blood, so he threw the roundhouse again because you never change a winning game and this time
it landed on the bigger man's nose and that started
bleeding and Amos realized he was a dead man now,
Freddy's fist, and Freddy charged, taking Amos with
him and they both smashed into the front door but in
the charge luckily Amos managed to lunge around so
even though Freddy had been the charger, Freddy
took the force of the collision and Amos heard the air
start to leave the big guy, a break, and boy could he
use any to forestall the inevitable, but in the mean-
time, while Freddy was getting his balance back,
Amos tried a jab, and to his stunned pleasure it found
Freddy's nose and immediately the blood began flowing more freely and Amos would have tried the nose
a third time except it hurt so damn much landing a

punch that he shifted his aim and winged a right
toward Freddy's stomach and my God, he must have
lucked into the proper balance because his first all but
disappeared and Freddy grunted and Amos liked the
sound, tried reproducing it with a left, succeeded. He
pounded with both hands now at Freddy's stomach,
getting in everything he could before Freddy launched
the inevitable attack that would destroy him, humil-
iate him in front of his once-wife, who had moved
now to the safety of the corridor, watching it all with
her bright green eyes, and Amos, in one final desperate attempt to put off his downfall, aimed a few at
Freddy's unprotected face and his right wasn't much
good but his left hit the lip again but that was all she
wrote because, open and unprotected himself now,
both punches thrown and balance gone, Amos caught
sight of Freddy's fist crashing toward his face and he
tried ducking to lessen the impact but the blow hit his
cheek and Amos stepped back a moment, assimilating
the effect of the blow, as for a brief isolated instant
the two of them stared at each other—

—hey—Amos realized—he's weaker than me—

—joyously, he leaped forward, throwing punches
wildly now, advancing on the dark-haired figure, who
began retreating around the foyer, shouting, "I'll kill
you—I'll kill you—I'll tear you fucking apart" and
Amos, awkwardly pursuing, said nothing, because the
energy of throwing the punches was winding him terribly but he got in a good one to the cheek and a hum-
mer on that nose again and Freddy was half running
now, around and around, with Amos in clutzy pursuit,
throwing everything he had, jabs like Sugar Ray, bolos
like Gavilan, and once, really showboating now, he
switched to southpaw, leading with his right, landing,
landing again, and Freddy was glancing toward the
hallway that led back to the master bedroom, which

spurred Amos into one final chopping effort and he
got in a straight right, smash on the mouth, and Christ
but Freddy had hard teeth but you couldn't let on
anything like that, so Amos didn't, being content instead to stare as the bigger man, demolished for all
practical purposes, clapped a hand over his mouth
and lumbered off out of sight down the corridor, past
Lila, who was standing there, rooted.

Amos returned her stare for a while, then, panting,
mimed a microphone. ". . . like tuh thank all my fans
. . . it were a tuff fight . . . but I always prides mahself
on stayin in condishun 'cuz I repree-zent the youff of
Ah-mahr-ica . . . an' thiss here is for my little lady . . ."
Amos blew a kiss in Lila's direction, then whipped the
mustache from his pocket, held it out.

Lila just stood there.

"Okay," Amos went on, his voice dead even. "Now
fix it!"

"Gimme the damn thing," Lila said, grabbing it from
his hand.

"Careful with that—"

Lila scowled at the mustache, muttering "Stupid
Pierre anyway," not always her attitude, since, as they
both well knew, Pierre had once been their semi-
salvation, at least for a time, immediately after the
Annie's Day firing, when Amos retreated whipped
from Philadelphia and had little else to do but sit
around the house and brawl with anyone in the vicinity, namely Lila. Sometimes the kid was present for
these tangles and on occasion when she was, one or
the other of them would try using her to prove them
right.

"Unlucky Pierre," Lila had said one night right after
dinner, as they cleared away the dishes, the two of
them, while the wee one got herself ready for bed.

"Meaning?" Amos asked.

"I don't know, but isn't there some joke about Lucky Pierre, always in the middle? Jessica's in the middle. We really must stop carping at each other, Amos. Look—just look—" she said then, holding up Jessica's plate. "That child is going to starve to death on East End Avenue."

"Maybe she ate a big lunch and wasn't hungry."

"I fed her lunch—she doesn't touch anything I cook her—"

"Maybe we should try restaurants—"

"—What you're saying is my cooking stinks, right?"

"Easy—"

"—I happen to be a good cook—any time you think you can do better—"

"—you say stop carping and then you start carping—"

"—it's not me, it's you, you're always at me—"

"—not tonight, sugarlump." Amos put down the dishes, threw on a sport coat, and left her there.

Forty minutes later, the doorbell to the apartment rang three quick times.

Lila answered it, started to say something, stopped.

"*Bonsoir,*" the man in the doorway said. He looked very much like Amos, except for a thick black mustache and a double boiler held tightly in one hand. His accent was heavily French. "*Je suis* looking for Monsieur Amos McCracken."

Lila started laughing. "What kind of stunt is this?"

"Zere is perhaps something funny?—I do not think so."

"—Amos—"

"*non*, madame—I look for Amos—*je suis* Pierre."

"Well I'm sorry, Pierre, but he stepped out."

Pierre shrugged. "The leetle one he has spoke of, she is step out too?"

"No, she's trying to get to sleep."

"*Bien*. Arouse her please. Tell her Pierre is come," which Lila did, informing her daughter of the visitor, who appeared a moment later, silent and strange in the doorway, the double boiler still in one hand. The other hand now held a large box of safety matches. Thus armed, he moved, still silent, toward the bed, reached it, stared at the child. "You slept?"

Jessica shook her head. "I had the insom; that's what my daddy calls it, he gets it too."

"*Naturellement*. He tell me of zis insom." Sitting on the child's bed, he lit a safety match, held it beneath the double boiler, his hand moving in slow circles.

"When did he tell you about his insom?"

"At the soccor match, *naturellement*."

"So*ccor?*—"

"—but surely he has speak of how we are in the same carton for the soccor match."

"He never said one single word." She sat up in bed now, peering through the match light at the mustached man. "Why is your mustache black and your hair almost blonde?"

"My beard is grey—there are many unanswered questions about me." He lit another kitchen match, again moved it in slow circles under the double boiler. "And I am very painful at your father."

"Very *painful?*"

"*Oui*. For not telling to you about the soccor game. Zat is an American expression, leetle one—to be painful at some person means when they do a thing that displease."

"Ohhh," Jessica said. "You mean 'sore' at. Daddy's always saying how he's sore at people." She began to laugh.

"Zere is perhaps something funny?—I do not think so. I use the wrong word?—I do not think so. Sore means painful, *oui?* Zerefore, I am painful at Amos for not having tell."

"Well, it does mean that, Pierre, but you don't say it."

"*Non,* leetle one, *you* don't say it, because being small, you have not the words. But do not be discourage, this Eeengleesh ees very rocky to learn."

"Hard to learn."

"Are not rocks hard?"

"Yes, but—"

"—just listen to me, Small, and soon you will *parle.*" He lit a third match, continued the circling.

"Why are you doing that?"

"Because when we sit in the carton, I remember Amos tell how your favorite food is a candy block called The Three Musketeers. I am very proud of how I speak—I speak more beautiful than anyone, don't you harmony?"

"Don't you *agree,* Pierre."

"Is not to be in harmony to be agree?" Suddenly Pierre stood up in the darkness. "—I go now—all you do is pick pick pick—good-bye. You have hurt my touches."

"Feel—" Jessica began and then stopped. "Don't go," she said then. "I never meant to hurt your touches. But I had the insom and when I have *that,* well it's just pick pick pick, ask Daddy."

Pierre hesitated.

"I promise not to correct you again," Jessica said.

"I do not mind if you correct me, Small. That is how we learn. But you only mistake me."

"I promise not to interrupt you again, I meant."

"*Bien,*" he said after a moment and sat down. "Where am I?"

"This is my bedroom," Jessica said.

Pierre shook his head. "*Sacre*—when I say 'where

am I' I don't mean 'where am I,' I know where I am,
I mean 'where am I'—in the history I tell."

"The Three Musketeers, you were talking about.
That certainly is my favorite."

"They steal it from us *naturellement*. The Americans. All the good food they steal from us."

"How do you know that?"

"*How do I know?* Because I am Pierre, the greatest
chef in all of France. Why do you think I am stop by
your house? I only cook for the rich and mighty and
tonight I am prepare the feast for the female horse of
all New York who live in Gracie House."

"You mean the Mayor?"

From the far dark corner, Lila began to laugh.

"Zere is perhaps something funny?—I do not think
so." Pierre began to rise again.

"Mommy, you *stop* that," Jessica said. "Please," she
told Pierre. "Everybody calls him the female horse. It's
just *terrible*. My teacher at school did it yesterday."

"Let me know if there's anything I can get you,
Pierre," Lila said, going.

"*Merci,* madame." He sat on the bed again. "Where
am I?"

"The Americans had stolen The Three Musketeers
from the French."

"You see? Already better. Before, you say 'in my
bedroom.' Now you are not so foolish. Just listen to
me, Small, and soon you will *parle*." He took the lid
off the double boiler, daintily reached inside, took out
a small chocolate-covered rectangle. "This is the original recipe zat the Americans steal." He handed the
candy to the child. "First, the Athos."

She nibbled at one corner. "It certainly tastes exactly like a Three Musketeers block."

"*Not better?*"

"Oh, no, much better, terrifically better, it's just

grreat, Pierre." and she popped the rest into her mouth.

"The Porthos and the Aramis are here when you wish." He pointed to the double boiler.

She nodded, looking very closely at him now. Her mouth still full and chewing, she managed, "Which exactly game did you meet my daddy?"

"It was all because of the WeeleeMay. I am in this country short jiffy and—"

"—ti—" she started, stopped.

"Something?"

"No, no, you were in this country short jiffy and what?"

"The WeeleeMay. It is summer, last, so everybody say the WeeleeMay come and he is *le plus,* so I go but he is very ovverrate—he cannot use his feet, he does not kick the ball, *terrible.* So I am very painful because to sit in a carton is not free and there is another there, cheering this WeeleeMay and I say to him, 'How can you cheer for a man who cannot kick the ball' and that *homme* was your, as you say, dah-dee, and—"

"But Daddy only goes to base—" She stopped, very excited suddenly. "It was a baseball game—Willie Mays—that's right, Daddy always goes to see Willie Mays."

"I just tell you that, do not repeat everything I tell you—"

"—can I have another piece of that French candy please?"

"Try the Aramis," he said, handing her another rectangle of chocolate. "Where am I?"

"You had just talked for the first time to Daddy."

"*Oui,* and he inform me that thees game we see is not soccor—"

"—is there more chocolate?"

"There is the Porthos." He handed her the last piece. "From there, your dah-dee and Pierre we vision that we are the same almost in appear, only *naturellement*, your dah-dee has no black mustache, and then we vision we like one the other, and we vision one the other for lunch when I am not work and I always promise I will stop by for *le dessert* if I am nearby which I am tonight since I work for the female horse —" He leaped up. "The female horse!—*sacre*—I am late—" and then he was out of the room, out the door, gone.

The next morning, while Amos was blowing at his coffee cup, Jessica walked into the kitchen. "Pierre was here," she said.

"You're yesterday's news, kiddo; your mother already told me. Why didn't he call first? I'd have cancelled my meeting if he'd called."

Jessica stared closely at her father.

"Something on my face?" Amos asked.

"No, no, but just where exactly did you meet him?"

Amos began to laugh. "That nut Frenchman—he thought baseball was soccer—he said, how can I cheer for Willie when he doesn't kick well. I figured oh-oh, they've let a loony into Shea, but then I realized he was just a foreigner who didn't understand. We look a lot alike, actually; except he's got that weirdo mustache."

Jessica nodded. "His beard is grey."

"He's gone and grown a *beard?*"

Jessica shook her head. "But if he did it would, he said so." She poured herself some orange juice. "I wonder if Mayor Lindsay liked him," she muttered then, and drank it down.

"*Why do you insult me?*" Pierre cried that night. "Tell me, Small. *Pourquoi?*"

"I didn't—I didn't—I just asked did he like the food you cooked, that's all."

"Am I not Pierre? Is it possible not to like my creations? *Non.* Why do you think I am back two nights jogging? Because the female horse, he beg me to return tonight and work my magic for the birth leaders."

"Who are they?"

"All the workers of the city belong to birth unions and they want more money and Leend-seey, he fear they may call a punch." He lit a match, circled it under his double boiler. "But after they have eat Pierre, no one can call a punch, Leend-seey know this, so he beg me." The match flame was the only light in the dark room, and the shadows swelled and died as it moved.

"Is that that grreat French candy?"

Pierre shook his head and began to whisper. "*Un* preview—for the birth leaders."

"What is it?"

He looked around the room a while, studying shadows. "We are absolutely alone? Spies from '21' pursue me night and day."

"There's only Mommy and she's watching the TV."

Pierre indicated the double boiler. "—for the first time in the new world—the great *spécialité* of Pierre —steak-chop—" and he took the lid from the double boiler, *voilà*'d a fork suddenly into his hand, jabbed it in. Then he held the fork close to her mouth, bits of meat clinging to the end of it. "Taste," he said. "Do not feel embarrass if you cry."

She took the food tentatively, rolled it round her mouth a moment, then said "grreat" and quickly chewed it down. "Whatever is it?"

"Your taste buds have die? You tell me."

"Well . . . it's sort of—" she ran her tongue across

her lips—"that really *is* great, Pierre, and it's sort of
. . . like lamb chop only sometimes it's steak."

"*Bon.* Perhaps you will make ze great chef, not great
like Pierre, but great." He jabbed another forkful, held
it out.

She gobbled it, wondering, "Do you cook them at
the same time or one after the other?"

Pierre jumped to his feet. "Nevair—zat is *absolument* the last time you will hurt my touches—"

"—what did I say?—"

"—you will nevair make ze great chef—"

"—well I'm only six—"

"—when I am six, I have already master hollandaise
sauce—"

"I only wanted to know if—"

"Small—did I not say it was a *spécialité?*—how
could it be *spécialité* of the greatest chef in all the
world if you take a steak and a chop and cook first the
one or first the other one or in the same pan or different—*non*—ze steak-chop belong to Pierre because
he is the only chef who make the steak-chop *with the
same piece of meat!*"

In the darkness, she stared up at him.

"She does not understand—Small, if you wish to be
the great chef, first you must use the brains—*écoute*
—in my *château* in France I get genius idea—I take a
big lamb and I breed with another big and get bigger
lamb, and I do that and do that and I also take a cow
and breed with bull that is runty and the lamb grow
and grow and the cow shrink and shrink and after
many year, when they are the same size, I mate, the
big lamb, the small cow. *Voilà*: steak-chop."

"Guess who cooked for me last night?" Jessica said
the next morning.

Amos looked up from Reston. "I'm just a little angry," he said. "If he's permanently working around here he should have told me."

"You had to go to your meeting but I got supper by Pierre. Guess what I had?"

"How'm I supposed to know? French candy again."

"No. Spaghetti. Pierre's special spaghetti."

"Did it have crushed-up bacon in it? He makes it that way sometimes he said—he always promised he'd let me try it but—"

"I had steak-chop," Jessica said then.

"*Steak-chop?*" Amos erupted. "That really bugs me. You don't know how much I've heard about this great thing he makes and how I'd cry tasting it it was so good and now you get it—you—he must have told me ten times about how he made it and then he gives it to a kid—ridiculous—a kid doesn't know how you make something like steak-chop—"

"It's just easy," Jessica said. "All you do is take a big lamb and a little cow and *voilà*."

"*Voilà*," Amos muttered, "I'll give ya *voilà*."

"*Au 'voir*, Small," Pierre said that night, standing beside the bed.

Jessica looked through the darkness at the mustached man. His hands were clasped in front of him. There was no double boiler. "Where are you going?"

"I am go no place—I stay in America but I cannot let you taste any more the *cuisine*."

"But why?"

"I only cook for food lovers, Small. Alas, you are not one."

"I ate every bit of the steak-chop—you saw."

"Small." He sat down beside her on the bed. "To eat Pierre's food is not to be a food lover—it only prove you are not die. But, I am come to admire you as a person, and *naturellement,* all the food people, they know Pierre—for me to make a purchase in their market makes them famous to each other—'he preferre my egg' they say to each other, 'he buy my *lemon'*— and I ask to see is your food the best and all the food people, they say, *'oui,* I send only the best food to *Monsieur* and *Madame* McCracken,' *'Et la petite Mc-Cracken?'* I ask, and they say, 'There are no children, only the two,' and I say *'non,* there are three' and they say *'non,* there cannot be three *parce que* I only send enough food for two' and I know, Small, that your *père* is fine at eating, and he tell me during our lunches how your *mère* is also fine, and so I cannot present you with more of my *cuisine,* because you do not eat, and if you do not eat, you cannot be a food lover, so *au 'voir,* Small." He stood up.

"I haven't been hungry lately."

Pierre shrugged.

"But I can feel my appetite coming back—I just get so I'm practically starving sometimes—"

"Talk, talk, talk—when the market men say there are three who live here, Pierre will know. It is strange, a child of Amos' turning out not to be a food lover. *Eh bien;* there must be many unanswered questions about you too."

Slowly, Pierre departed. And the next night he did not return. And life went back much to what it had been, but with at least one fairly startling development.

The kid believed.

"You're crazy," Amos said.

Lila rolled up to one elbow on the bed. "Cross my heart."

"She's too smart, for God's sake."

"I'm telling you, Amos, it's not just that she's eating all of a sudden like a piglet, she's always asking me questions about him. Do I think Pierre knows she finished her soup at lunch? How will Pierre find out about the seconds on stew?"

"You really honest Injun think she believes?" He lay on his back and began drumming on his kneecaps. "It's been a week since his last visit." He turned off his bed lamp and rolled onto one side, away from Lila, staring out at the late October night. "Maybe there is something to it—she's always trying to catch me up with inconsistencies—tonight she asked wasn't it lucky I went to see Carl Yastrzemski or I never would have met Pierre? Now where the hell did she hear about Carl Yastrzemski?"

"Lorenzo."

"Who?"

"He's got this mad crush on her in kindergarten. Lorenzo's father's a Yastrzemski fan."

"What kind of a father would call his kid Lorenzo? Does she like this Lorenzo?"

"Considering that one of them's a boy and the other isn't and they're both six, yes." She turned off her bed lamp. "Now I'm not saying she one-hundred-percent nail-me-to-the-cross believes, but it's a lot more than fifty-fifty. I think it's like Santa Claus; she's afraid not to believe. I mean, who can face those consequences?"

"She really likes Pierre, wouldn't you say?" He began drumming on Lila's leg.

"I hate it when you do that—use your own kneecaps—"

"—sorry—"

"—as far as can be determined, she is mad for him—" Amos cackled in the night. . . .

Pierre arrived the next evening with French strawberry cheesecake in his double boiler, and whenever he appeared after that, which was often in those late October–early November days, he was never greeted with less than joy. Jessica not only always finished whatever he brought her, she in addition was downing most of what was set on her plate three meals a day, so the childhood eating problem, which had once loomed so large, was now nil, which could not be said of some of the difficulties belonging to the grownups in the family, and after the anniversary split, resulting in Amos' hotel move, Pierre appeared less and less in everybody's life. But some nights he did come, a little softer of speech now, a little less linguistically temperamental, sitting silently on some occasions, but on others after prodding, he would talk of many things; old loves, new tastes, triumphs and pâtés, roasts and tears. . . .

"Here!" Lila announced, snapping the excess thread away, shoving the mustache back at Amos. "And have her back by supper and don't stuff her with candy."

Amos inspected Lila's handiwork. "Really a good job." He pulled gently at the mustache and the nose clip, testing. "Like new, thanks." He pocketed it.

Lila walked quickly to the front door, yanked it open. "By supper, Amos; don't screw around, got that?"

"Right, right." He started toward the elevator. "Hey —does she know Nathan's has opened a branch on Forty-third Street?"

"No, Amos, she doesn't, and if Pavillon's been sold again, she doesn't know that either, why do you ask things like that? You're really getting crazy—*crazier,* I should say."

Amos shrugged, blew his ex a kiss. "They said the same thing about Nero."

iii

Even though Jessica was only six, kindergarten was her fourth year at Cannon School, a circumstance brought on by Lila's pediatrician, who felt that the child was the kind who would benefit from the classroom experience.

"Benefit from the classroom experience?" Amos had shouted. "She's *two*, what's she gonna major in, eurhythmics?"

"I'm just repeating—" Lila began, but Amos would have none of it.

"—Jesus, Lila, what if we're too late—I mean, suppose she's behind all the others who've been hitting the books since they turned one? What kind of a classroom experience will that be for the kid, two years old and already a whole year behind?"

"You can crack wise all you want to, I have tuned out."

"I wonder if they give a good course in toilet training?"

"They have to be toilet trained," Lila said. "Jessica still makes mistakes and I hope that doesn't ruin her chances."

"You mean you've checked this thing out seriously?"

"The two most convenient would be Dalton or Cannon. Dalton may be too progressive—"

Amos put his hands over his ears.

"Amos, this just might be the most crucial event in your child's life."

Her sincerity stopped him. He dropped his hands, waited.

Lila hurried on. "Here's the thing—if she goes to Dalton, that's through high school and if she does decent work at all, which she will, since God knows she's nothing if not verbal and they're very big on that at Dalton, then she's practically a cinch for Radcliffe, Wellesley or Bryn Mawr—Dalton's got good ins there. And Cannon, well Cannon's only through eighth grade but they've got good ins with Chapin and Brearley for high school and Chapin and Brearley have both got good ins with Radcliffe, Wellesley and Bryn Mawr."

"The one that's asleep thumb-sucking in her crib, we're talking about?"

Lila nodded. "Oh, Amos, you do see? I know it's expensive but it could be just so important." She came into his arms. "If Jessica ends up going to some state school and it's our fault, Amos, how are we going to live with ourselves? I mean that."

Amos looked at her stunning face. She did mean it, and it baffled him, but he was a Middle-Western foreigner while she was a townie, a rich and social one, whose refusal to be a debutante had rocked her family's foundations and her subsequent decision to attend Wellesley over Sweet Briar had practically sent her bitch mother into Menninger's, so Amos ceded to her wisdom. "Okay, okay, I give; which do we pick, Dalton or Cannon?"

Lila looked at him amazed. "Pick? We don't pick. My God, don't you know anything? They select."

Eventually, after tension-filled interviews, after tests for children and insults for everyone, after every conceivable string had been pulled and pulled again, Cannon came through and off the wee one went to get educated. The entire decision-making process was so horrendously unstringing that Amos could still not

approach the place without a slight tightening of the
stomach wall, a perceptible beating of the heart.

At precisely ten-twenty-eight, he crossed the street
toward Cannon School, on-the-button perfect timing,
the only kind when you were dealing with Miss
Bacon, who was every bit as compulsive about the
clock as he was. Amos gave his all to please Miss
Bacon since (a) he was crazy about her and (b) she
was equally enthused about the kid. She had taught
Jessica in nursery school, and among the good things
that had happened the fall preceding was that Miss
Bacon moved up to kindergarten, graduating, more or
less, with her class. She was quite young, under thirty,
with sufficient hours for her doctorate and a face that
was Doris Day pretty, both facts she did her best to
hide, the first by silence, the second by flab. She was
totally and unnecessarily blimplike, and Amos sometimes wondered what kind of job her folks must have
done on her to bring about the disfigurement.

Amos entered Cannon. It was remarkable that so
much blood was annually spilled to gain admission to
two such crummy buildings, adjoining brownstones in
the East Eighties, between York and First. Miss
Bacon's room was the lead door on the left, and at
ten-thirty all the fathers milled in. The classroom itself was quite large and well lit and the fifteen children sat in a semicircle in the farthest corner. At a
nod from Miss Bacon, they got up and fled toward
their fathers and Amos, watching Jessica come to him,
realized with some joy that he had never seen her
looking quite as well, her Lahr face decidedly in retreat, and although it was conceivable that her next
resemblance might be Jimmy Cagney, there was some
chance she might not turn out to be homely after all.
At least not old-maid-style homely.

She curtsied in her somber way before him, saying,

the practice plain, "Thank you for coming to our party," and Amos bowed gravely back, saying, "To tell you the truth, Miss Bacon, my kid's always told me how young you were but this is ridiculous," and she said, "Daddy—" but he rambled on, working for the smile with "—and I had no idea you were so short, you could actually pass for one of your students," to which she answered, "Yes, that's so, everybody's always saying that." They shook hands then, embraced then, and he held her high.

When he put her down, she returned to the semi-circle, sitting as ladylike as possible on the floor, where a moment later a scruffy little male clambered around and pushed his way in beside her, clearly, Amos realized, Lorenzo. When all fifteen were in place, Miss Bacon sat in a child's chair before them, tapped a wooden pencil lightly against the linoleum floor for quiet, raised a hand and then, hesitant and pure, came the glorious sexless sound of the young in song.

> *"By thy rivers gently flowing,*
> *Illinois, Illinois . . .*
> *By thy prairies verdant growing,*
> *Illinois, Illinois . . .*
> *Comes an echo from the years,*
> *Abraham Lincoln's name appears,*
> *Grant and Logan and our tears,*
> *Illinois, Illinois . . .*
> *Grant and Logan and our tears,*
>   *Illinois . . ."*

Amos' quirky mind, paranoid as it admittedly was, was in no way ready for *that* song, and as its power blindsided him, back he tumbled where he never much wandered any more, into his frigid Illinois boyhood, where they always sang that great crappy song

at assembly and how many times had he wondered
and asked who Logan was, since he must have been
important, getting two mentions in the song while
Abe had to content himself with one. But nobody was
too big on Logan, it was just one of those mysteries
like did the Babe really point to center field and call
the homer or was he just gesturing with the bat and—

"... *Abraham Lincoln's name appears ...*"

—and Amos, rooted in Cannon, was pushing thirty-
three and divorced and dear God, how old had his old
man been when his mother took off? Less than thirty-
three? Had to be, because his old man was only thirty-
nine when he as they say made his ultimate departure
shattering all medical records by being the only man
in the history of Athens, Illinois to kick off from an excess of acidity in the soul and—

"... *Grant and Logan and our tears ...*"

—and Amos stared at his ugly sweetheart and would
she be divorced too by the time she was his age and
would she run off with some destructive stranger and
were there such things as family curses, were the Mc-
Crackens for some ancient sin forever to roam the
earth, unable to live painlessly with others and there
had to be a release from it somewhere, it couldn't be
Sisyphean, not even God was that cruel, somehow the
stone had to balance on the top of the hill but what
was the secret, how did you make it stay, maybe if
you did enough bad things, maybe if you gathered all
the guilt available on the North American continent
He would have at last mercy and say 'Leave the Mc-
Crackens the hell alone,' and—

"... *Illinois* ..."

As the song ended Amos groped for a child's chair and sat, feeling much like a James Bond Martini, shaken and chilled. The surrounding fathers clapped loudly and he managed to throw his hands together and then Miss Bacon was talking to the fifteen, talking as always, to them not at them, her voice low.

"Why did we sing that song today?" she asked.

"Because our daddies are here," Lorenzo replied immediately.

"That's certainly *a* reason, Lorenzo, but why that particular song—"

"—because—" Lorenzo began.

"—please remember about raising your hands," Miss Bacon said. "Now we've talked about that all year, and I know it's hard but we simply must do it. All right, Lorenzo, raise your hand and then you can talk."

Lorenzo raised his hand. "Because you taught it to us."

Giggles from the class.

The *dunce*, Amos thought. Jesus. What the hell can she see in him? He peered at the child bouncing beside his daughter. Nice enough looking but a little on the small side. Amos looked closer. He wasn't a little small, he was a runt, so why—omigod, Amos realized: it's because she's mothering him. Six years old and already she's decided on her place in life; nobody's lover, everybody's pal. It must have been the divorce that changed her—she was never like that when he was around.

"That certainly is true, Lorenzo, I did teach it to you, but I think we're straying from the point. Chris?"

"Lincoln came from Illinois," everybody said, in something resembling unison.

"He was murdered," Lorenzo said then.

"That's right, he certainly was, and we'll get to that, Lorenzo," Miss Bacon said, unruffled and adored and Amos thought that if they bottled her disposition and sold it at drugstores, would he ever lay in a supply.

"Actually," Robin said, after raising her hand, "he was born in Kentucky," Robin being Jessica's best girl friend, another blabber, a pretty little button of a child, fair and spookily scientific. Instead of dolls she messed with screwdrivers and whenever she came to the apartment to play, you always had to check, after her departure, to see that the light plugs weren't lying dismembered near their sockets.

"He was indeed, very good, Robin," Miss Bacon replied. "Lincoln was born in eighteen-hundred and nine and . . ."

Amos sat forward suddenly, because the terrible wrinkled look had taken over his kid's face, and he wondered what in the world was going on inside.

"Yes, Jessica, what is it?" Miss Bacon asked, responding from experience to the look.

"You could have taught us 'My Old Kentucky Home' then, if you'd wanted."

Miss Bacon nodded. "Yes, that's true, and knowing you, Jessica, what you're really wondering is why I didn't teach you 'My Old Kentucky Home'?"

Jessica nodded.

"I don't know," Miss Bacon said. "I honestly do not. And if *I* don't know all the answers, then there's no reason for *you* to know them either, so if you ever get stuck, don't feel unhappy about it, is that clear to everyone, Robin and Jessica?"

Amos nodded along with the two, remembering the despair that immediately clutched the kid whenever she goofed on something she felt she shouldn't have, and Robin was the same.

"Now Lincoln went to Illinois and he became a . . . ?"

The ensemble was evenly divided between "rail splitter" and "lawyer."

"Everybody wins on that one," Miss Bacon said, shifting her blimp shape into another position. "He went into local politics and then what happened to him when he left Illinois?"

"He got shot," Lorenzo said.

"You're awfully morbid this morning, Lorenzo, why is that do you think?"

Lorenzo hadn't the least idea.

"Morbid means?" Miss Bacon waited. "Anybody?— guess—"

"Dum-dum" was the first suggestion.

"Not exactly. Another guess, come on—"

"Yukky?"

"Yukky is closer than dum-dum but not quite it yet —now we all are crazy about a certain morbid animal and he had a birthday party and he got a torn balloon and an empty honey jar and—"

"Eeyore!" half a dozen shouted.

"Right. Eeyore. And what was Eeyore always being?"

"Gloomy," from two-thirds.

"Right. So 'morbid' means—"

"*Gloomy,*" came from all the throats.

Miss Bacon nodded, tapped her pencil on the floor. "Now in eighteen-sixty, Lincoln was elected—"

"—President!"

"And in eighteen-sixty-one came the?—"

"—Civil War."

"And in eighteen-sixty-three came the?—"

Everybody did the best they could with "Emancipation Proclamation."

"And in eighteen-sixty-four he was re-elected, and this question is just for you, Lorenzo, what happened to Lincoln in eighteen-sixty-five?"

"He was shot in the movies," Lorenzo replied.

Uproar from the others.

Under the din Miss Bacon said, "Now that's not all that bad an answer—it's not quite right, but why isn't it?" and as she went on, the class quieted to her. "Why isn't it ri—Jessica, are you whispering Lorenzo the answer?"

"Well he's missed so many."

"What did she whisper to you, Lorenzo?"

"They didn't have movies yet."

"What else didn't they have?—anybody—just name things—"

"—TV—"

"—airplanes—"

"—potties—"

"No," Miss Bacon said. "They had potties, just not indoors."

"Yuk," Lorenzo said.

"My sentiments exactly," Miss Bacon said, an expression of hers, and they all began giggling before it was over and Amos, sitting with the passing time, had few complaints as they associated from Lincoln to other things and back and then the fathers were served juice and cookies and snacked with their own, and then it was speech time, and all the students gave prepared texts ranging up to fifteen seconds in length on the subject of their daddies, telling their names and hobbies and anything else of general interest and the kid bushwhacked Amos, mentioning to his unhappy surprise about how he played tunes on his kneecaps, a situation he tried to suave his way through as the other ancients looked at him and somehow suddenly it was noon, time to put everything away and as the children got into their clothing by themselves, Amos moved to Miss Bacon by the door and said he'd seen many less enjoyable shows on

Broadway and she thanked him and he asked, "How are things?" meaning with Jessica, but her answer was, "Weary and tense, I suppose."

"Well listen," Amos said. "After putting your charges through something like this, who wouldn't be?" He lowered his voice then. "I meant with you know."

"So did I," Miss Bacon said, shaking hands with the first father out the door, waving to the child that went with him.

Jessica was still getting into her things, making sure her hair was straight and Amos stood by the door of the emptying room, looking at Miss B., the two of them getting in their euphemisms as best they could.

"That's not so red hot, is it?" Amos said.

"Not so very." She shook more hands, waved and waved again.

"But, like, it's a very gradual thing, wouldn't you say?"

"No, actually, it's been getting to be quite a sharp descent of late." She faced the door. "Good-bye . . . good-bye . . ."

"How can things be bettered?"

"I wish to hell I knew, Amos," Miss Bacon said, her spherical face dead on him. She took a step away from the door, toward a final privacy, and pointed to nothing in particular on the wall. "It's really quite a remarkable piece of baggage, you know—but it needs such gentle handling, and I'm worried the corners are already starting to cave—"

"Hi," Jessica said.

"We'll be shoveling off," Amos said to the fat lady. "See you." He turned to the kid. "It was grreat," he told her, pleased he had remembered before she could get out the question. They headed for the door.

At the doorway, Jessica turned to her teacher,

waved, then dashed out of the building calling "I'm
the leader" to Amos, a habit she had had since she
could dash. Amos caught up with her on the sidewalk.
"Whose day is it," Jessica asked him, "mine or yours?"

"Yours."

"And anything I want to do I get to do?"

"I guess," Amos said. He usually let her have one or
two 'days' a year, and all it ever amounted to was eating in a restaurant and then hitting a Broadway show
or a flick if there weren't matinees. Amos preferred to
go to Broadway, since for the last two years Jessica
had always asked to se *Francie,* of which she never
tired, thereby making him something of a big deal, and
sitting happily time after time through the good parts
as well as those not so cockle warming. The kid must
have caught *Francie* ten times by now, which was
certainly gratifying, but more than that, when he,
Amos, had been a kid back in Athens, Illinois and had
saved his shekels over the months so he could take the
North Shore into Chi and catch a road company, his
father had put a stop to it because the tall bitch who
lived across the street told his old man that letting
Amos see shows would spoil him 'blase'—Amos never
heard that word without seeing the mouth across the
street forming it—and Amos' father heeded the pig's
wisdom. So Amos, right or wrong, loved to take Jessica to shows, since when she enjoyed herself, which
she did always, he was consciously slipping it to the
tall bitch who still lived in his mind across the street
from him, and who had curtailed with her lip much
of the charm of his adolescence.

"I wanna have some food and then I wanna go to
theodore," this last her word for 'theatre' before she
could pronounce it properly, and which he enjoyed,
so they kept it current between them.

They walked slowly toward First Avenue. The day

was heating up still, almost freakishly warm for mid-February now, and beautiful. "Deal," Amos said.

"Grreat, can I be the leader to the corner?" and she took off after Amos' nod, racing between the old houses, with surprising speed for a young body, and Amos reflected that maybe she might have a chance to settle down with someone decent after all in fifteen years or so, no matter how homely her face might eventually become; a lot of girls went places on good bodies. Of course, she'd have to have a bit more breast than her mother, or you could just cash in now. What chance was there if you had no head and a body like a desk top? Who was going to stick in your vicinity long enough to check out what your mind might be? There were bust developers in movie magazines but they were all phony; the developers and the hormone creams were worth zippo; it was what The Old Man gave you, and besides, the kid was only six, so why fill your mind with garbage now, especially since in ten years they might have a bust cream that really worked; hell, if they could land on the goddam moon, what was so tough about swelling a few boobies? "Hey guess what?" she called from the corner.

Amos walked up to her. "I give. What?"

"Lorenzo has a penis."

Immediately aware of being on shaky ground, Amos managed "Zat so" and fell silent.

"So does his daddy."

"That's sure nice," Amos said. "Hey, here's the thing about lunch—"

"So do you, right?"

"Right, right." Amos took her hand to cross First Avenue and while they walked he wondered why didn't they ever let you know when they were going to unload on you with something on sex or race or why was everybody killing everybody. If they could only learn to give clues, then you could prepare, launch yourself toward the nearest Spock, flip through blessed Selma Fraiberg, really prepare yourself, so that when the fatal questioning came, you could be boned up and give a coherent, meaningful answer, instead of stumbling through the quicksand, hoping you weren't loosing any traumas, then madly changing the subject, whether the opportunity presented itself or no.

"Well why *do* you?"

Amos wasn't quite sure what the antecedent was, so he just shrugged.

"It just seems to me that all the boys have all the penises."

"Well, that's true, in a manner of speaking, yes."

"Well why don't I have one?"

"You're only six—what in the world would you want one for?"

"I'll never have one—Robin found out and told—no matter how old I get—why don't mommies have them is what I wanna know."

Some mommies do, Amos was about to answer, thinking naturally of his one and only Lila, but thank God he caught his tongue because if the words had gotten airborne, sooner or later Jessica would have mentioned it and then oh then the phone call: *'Did you tell Jessica I had a penis?'*—'No, Lila, I only . . .' —'I don't like you cracking wise about my superstructure, ya got that?'—'The child was naturally curious, Lila, and all I said was . . .'—*'Well, I just told her yours was made of Silly Putty, sweat that one out, you bastard!'*—

"Pasta!" Amos said.

"What, Daddy?"

"For lunch—that's what I want, it just hit me, some

nice steaming ravioli maybe, all crammed full of gar-
lic, what do you say?"

"Well . . ."

"Forget it, it's your day—I tell you what I'd really
like, fish. Nice fresh fish stew, how's that sound?"

"I'm not so crazy about fish yet."

"Wait—*wait*—have I got an idea, you'll die—"

"What?"

"Some of the world's greatest hot dogs—your favorite—Nathan's!"

"Nathan's?" She began bobbing up and down.

"Yes—we'll zoom out to Coney Island and have us
a feast."

"Grreat. *Grreat.*"

"Oh," Amos said then. He stopped suddenly as they
were moving up toward Second Avenue. "We can't."

"Why?"

"No time, baby, see?" He showed her his watch.
"It's going on twelve-thirty and it's an hour out there
easy and another hour back not to mention the time
we eat and by then the matinees'll practically be over."

"Couldn't we somehow?"

"I never should have brought it up, sorry." He
walked slowly along. "If there was only some way we
could do both. I said you could do both, I feel so
rotten going back on my word." He stopped again,
peering intently down at her. Then he shook his head.
"Naw, it'd never work."

"What wouldn't?"

"Forget it."

"Tell me."

"You'd just laugh."

"Please."

"Well . . ." He almost said something, shook his
head.

"Go *on.*"

"If it didn't work, I'd feel so stupid, I've never even tried doing it before."

"Doing what, doing what?"

Amos checked to see if they were alone on the sidewalk. Then he said it soft: "Architectural transference."

"What's that?" She moved up right alongside him.

Amos dropped to his knee. "Remember when me and Mommy went to London for the *Francie* opening?"

Jessica nodded.

"Remember me telling you about the Tibetan guru that took a liking to us?"

Jessica shook her head.

Amos stood up. "Well you just never pay attention and it really gets to me sometimes—I told you all about him and now you say 'no.'"

"But you didn't, never, never."

"Okay, it's your day. I'll take your word for it." He squatted down on his knee again. "Now what's our problem? We want to eat at Nathan's, but it's in Coney Island and by the time we get there, we can't go to the theodore because it's in Times Square, right?"

"Right, right."

"Well naturally, this sort of thing happens to everybody all over, but in Tibet they've whipped it. Like this guru was stuck at this crucial business meeting at the IBM building in the heart of Lhasa, while outside of town they were holding the Himalayan Cup, which is practically the Wimbledon of mountain climbing. So what he did of course was to solve his problem with architectural transference."

"But what *is* it?"

Amos shook his head. "I don't know though—that guru had years of practice. Except he did promise I could do it the first time if I concentrated properly. That's the whole ball game: total concentration."

"Daddy, I don't understand anything."

Amos glared at the child. "You just cannot put two and two together *ever*. Obviously architectural transference means that if I do it right, I'll be able to bring Nathan's from Coney Island to Times Square and that way we'll be able to do both, have a leisurely lunch and then go on to the theodore."

"Move Nathan's?" She began to giggle.

"I told you you'd laugh, the incident's shut, let's go have some nice fish."

"I'm not laughing, see? Really, Daddy, I promise I won't make a sound."

"It's all right, go ahead. I can't do it anyway, there's something I forgot—see, in order for architectural transference to work, you've got to have a good open space to land whatever it is you're moving, you can't just have one building going clump on top of another, people might get hurt, and there's no open space in Times Square, so . . ."

"Times Square, so—go on—see how I'm listening?"

"There is an open space in Times Square—where they tore down the old Astor Hotel on Forty-fifth Street—it's gigantic and plenty of room to land Nathan's. What I'd give for that guru to be here for just two minutes."

"But you said he told you how."

"Yeah, but how do I know he wasn't putting me on? —some joker of a guru trying to make me look bad in front of my kid."

"*Try.*" She was bobbing up and down faster than before.

"What if I can't make it happen? You'll laugh again and—"

"I never would, I promise—you try and if it doesn't work we'll just eat fish that's all."

"Okay." Amos took a deep breath. "I feel like an

idiot." He closed his eyes. "Nathan's," he whispered. ". . . Nathan's . . . Nathan's . . . come to Manhattan, Nathan's . . . I'm concentrating all my attention on you, Nathan's, so transfer yourself to where the Astor used to be on Forty-fifth Street, Nathan's . . . now, Nathan's . . ." Amos stopped abruptly and looked around, embarrassed. "I can't do it," he said. "I didn't feel a thing. I must not have concentrated hard enough." He continued on Second Avenue, Jessica several paces behind.

She moved up alongside. "Listen, the thing of it is—"

"—*omigod!*" Amos cried, clutching his head suddenly, staggering back, slamming hard against the side of the nearest brownstone. His eyes went wide and his mouth was working strangely: "NAY . . . NAY . . . NAYTH . . ." His voice died, his body sagged against the building. He began to pant as his arms fell like sticks to his sides.

"Daddy—what?" she began, running to him.

Amos just gasped, unable to speak.

"Daddy, I wish—"

". . . craziest thing . . ." Amos managed. ". . . wild . . . like I could feel things moving inside my head . . ."

"I think you were trying to say Nathan's."

"When?"

"Just now, don't you remember?"

"There was this blinding thing hit me . . . must be some new kind of virus . . ." he pushed himself away from the brownstone, started slowly to try to walk.

"Daddy, I really do think we should go right to the Astor Hotel."

"What, are you kidding?"

"*You were under a spell, Daddy*, I could see that."

"A spell, huh?"

She was really bobbing now. "It was just exactly

like on the cartoons—the way you held your head and then your eyes going all wide and staring and the crazy way you talked. There's just no question it was a spell and I think we would be making the most horrible kind of mistake if we didn't even take a peek at the Astor, Daddy."

"Well, there's no harm taking a peek, I suppose—I mean, we have to hit that area sooner or later, so—" He hailed a cab, asked for Forty-fifth Street and Broadway and rubbed his eyes. "Wow, that was sure some kind of crazy virus attack." "If it was Nathan's, I'm gonna have a hot dog—" "—If it was Nathan's I'm gonna have two hot dogs—" "Right, right, two hot dogs and the French fries—" "Well, it's all pie in the sky but of course we'll both have the French fries and the orange drink—" "and not the little orange drink, the huge—" Amos closed his eyes. "We'll both have the huge, baby, but I really feel kind of strange, like I'm getting sick, so you just tell me when we get there." He sat back in the seat, feeling the kid's rhythmic bobbing up and down, up and down, as slowly, through the matinee traffic, they made their way to where the Astor used to be.

"I don't quite see it yet," she said, as Amos paid the driver.

They got out and she took his hand as he led her across the sidewalk, moving against the grain of pedestrian traffic, until they stood at the edge of the great square of rubble. Amos stared out straight ahead. "It didn't work," he said finally. "I'm sorry."

"We mustn't be too hasty, Daddy." She scanned the rubble, her head moving back and forth, taking it all in. "Just think how horrible we'd feel if we missed it." She continued looking here, there, strafing the field with her eyes.

"Baby, there's nothing, no Nathan's."

"Let me just look one more time."

"No point. Let's go get some fish."

"Well . . ."

"C'mon." He yanked at her arm twice, like a train whistle. "I wonder if the halibut's fresh today?— you'll learn to like fish, it just takes time—"

"I like tuna fish."

"Right, right—and this place down a ways has the best hot tuna fish aspic in town. Comes to the table rippling like blubber. It's a real treat. And they serve these sensational turnips. Plus, get this now, rutabagas."

Jessica nodded, staring around as they walked downtown.

"And the dessert—oh that Fish Palace Special; that's the name of the place we're going to, the Fish Palace."

"Why is it so special?"

"In the first place, it's the only dessert they serve, and in the second place, nobody else has the recipe. Nope, if you want shrimp ice cream you've just gotta head for the Fish Palace."

Jessica stared around faster now as they moved.

"See, it looks maybe like just ordinary vanilla from a distance, but once you sink your spoon into it you realize that there's shreds of fresh shrimp meat imbedded throughout—"

"—Daddy!—"

"—honey, you know not to point, and this shrimp ice cream I'm telling you—"

"—Nathan's, Daddy, Nathan's—"

"—we can't get there in time, remember?—"

"—*look!*—" and she pointed desperately down to the corner of Forty-third Street.

Amos stopped, followed her gesture, turned back to the empty Astor space, then to Forty-third Street again, then down to his daughter, muttering, "It couldn't have been architectural transference," and after he shook his head he managed, "but what the hell," and suddenly he was all action, grabbing the child up, starting to run through the traffic, down and across the ugly intersection, and when they reached the place in they went, having each a hot dog flooded with mustard and the huge orange drink plus splitting an order of French fries and then, casually, carefully, taking their half-drunk drinks so that none of the precious fluids spilled, they took the stairs down to the lower level where there were duplicate food stations and again they ordered franks and another plate of fries and a butter-smeared corn ear in case anyone felt like nibbling and, after some philosophical discussion it was generally agreed upon that the French fries were better upstairs but the hot dogs better down and why was that, the chef or the ingredients or the cooking equipment, and as they sat lazily in the basement, preparing for dessert, Jessica said, "You didn't really make Nathan's move."

Amos stretched. "I didn't say I did." He got up, headed for the custard-cone department. "As a matter of fact, I specifically denied that architectural transference was in any way responsible. Van or choc?"

"Choc."

"Two chocolates," Amos said to the coneman. "And my mother here would like hers rare." He glanced down at the kid. "Hey, speaking of your mother—"

"—I'll just have to ask Robin about that spell of yours. Robin has a book with a chapter on spells—"

"—speaking of your mother," Amos went on casually, "I met that new friend of hers, what's his name?"

Jessica shrugged and shook her head.

"You know, the big guy, dark." Amos paid for the cones, handed one over.

Jessica shook her head again.

Amos led the way to the paper napkins, wrapped one around her cone, then his. "Seems like a nice fella, actually—Ferd I think his name was."

Jessica licked her cone carefully, concentrating on it.

"You want to eat these in or out?" Amos asked.

Jessica aimed her cone toward the up escalator.

"I didn't spend much time with them, to tell you the truth, but from what I could tell, Ferd came over A-O.K."

Jessica hopped onto the bottom stair of the escalator.

Amos followed the wee one on the ascent. God but she was tough to crack sometimes. He glanced at his watch. It was getting on to matinee time and if he was going to garner any poop, now was the only chance possible, since he could never bring the subject up again, that would be making too much of it, because maybe she'd mention his snooping to Lila and he couldn't stand the thought of Lila's gloating, even if he had put Frederick A. Hunter in his hip pocket no more than four hours before. Amos sighed, continuing to drill away. "He's taken quite a liking to you, I bet. Ferd, I mean."

"Fred."

"Right, right," Amos licked his cone. "Fred Huntley."

"Hunter, and really, Daddy, you must learn to listen when names are given."

They eased out of Nathan's. "Well put." Amos glanced down at her. She was concentrating on her cone again but Amos felt the nervousness anyway. "He really is crazy about you. It sounded like you two were practically playmates."

She shrugged.

"I guess he must kind of spend his days with you and Mommy, so I guess you and Mommy must want him to."

She was getting edgier now. "Isn't it about time?" she asked.

"For theodore? Close to it. Old Fred, he didn't seem quite as blabby as you and me, but I guess Mommy doesn't mind the change."

"Can I pick?"

"You always do."

"The new one," she said then. *"Annie's Day."*

"Next time," Amos answered, understanding her nervousness now. "I don't feel like seeing that show."

"Mommy said it was gonna close so I should be sure and see it now."

"She said that, did she? She's such a theatrical expert, suddenly. I'm amazed she can spare the time to study Broadway's ups and downs with Freddy Hunter around so much."

"He's not around so much and you said I could pick."

"A lot though, am I correct? Day and night?" Amos told himself to stop.

"You said. Anything I wanted."

"How 'bout those nights?"

"I really do think it might be fun for me to see it."

"Catch it at its first revival, kiddo. Freddy said he loved having breakfast with you. Is he a big eater or just coffee?"

"Just coffee—please, Daddy, I very much want to see the other show. Mommy bought me the record so I'm sure I'll understand just everything."

"How come he stops by for breakfast?—he must be some kind of early riser or does he live in the building, probably that's it—" *Let her off the hook.*

"—I don't know, Daddy, please—"

"—quit bugging me about it, you're not gonna see it—"

"—but you did say—"

"—finish your cone!—don't you know not to pester grownups?—gimme the damn thing," and he ripped it from her hand and dumped both in the nearest garbage can. "Wipe the chocolate off your mouth—"

"—you're going to make me about to cry—"

"—whine away—" and he signaled a taxi—"I mean, what am I arguing with a six-year-old about going to theatre for on a beautiful day—no kid should go to theatre, you're too young anyway, don't you know that, you keep on going to theatre it'll spoil you blasé now get in!" and he threw the cab door open, boosted her across the seat, followed her, slammed the door, told the driver Central Park. The taxi got to Sixth, made a left, began to move uptown. "There's no point in crying," Amos said to his daughter's back.

She faced him. "I'm not."

Amos licked his index finger, made a mark in the air.

"I've been working on my crying lately."

"—you want I should go into the park?—" from the driver.

"Please."

The car entered the masterpiece, which was not at its best, the month being what it was; still, the day almost compensated for the lack of leaves. When they came to an especially stunning turn, Amos told the man to let them out, paid, and then he and the kid took up walking.

It was weird. There was no one. Cars, yes, but the shocking heat of the day was having some kind of delayed reaction on the locals. Tomorrow probably, when the temp was down in the thirties, they would hit the place in waves, since yesterday was a winner, but now, it was almost like private grounds. "This is really good for us," Amos said. "It would have been stupid to spend a day like this inside."

"Why are we the only smarties?"—her word for those possessed of wisdom, its opposite being a dumdum.

"Because everyone in Manhattan tests very high on suspicion. Right now, all over town people are saying to each other, 'I hear it's nice out today,' and the answer is 'Who says? I hear it's gonna turn rainy' and while they discuss the value of their sources, the day goes." He pointed to a playground up on a rise, oval and empty. "You can swing me," he told her, as they started for it.

"Don't you want to know how I'm working on my crying?"

He nodded.

"Well, Robin had this traumatic experience with her daddy when he screamed at her that she was crying too much and he was going to count how often and, well, naturally, that just made her cry right on the spot and he said, 'One!' and she told me all about it the next morning, and, well, we got to talking and I wondered how much we cried, how many times and, well you know how interested in numbers Robin is, so Robin and I, well, we decided to test in secret and find out and tell each other and then we made a game out of it and whoever winned got to borrow a Kiddle for the next week, and, well, I was so afraid Robin might take my Kiddle apart to see how it worked I decided to stop crying. I just haven't lost yet. I'm not winning so much either though, on account of Robin stopped too, except sometimes when her daddy screams at her about taking apart the light plugs."

They paused at the edge of the deserted playground.

There was one man, a drunk most likely, dozing face
to the sun on a bench outside the fence beyond the
swings. Other than that, no one. Amos bowed con-
summately. "Shall we?"

She hesitated. "I wonder if there are any sticky
bugs."

Amos sighed. Sticky bugs were her third great fear,
following fire, which was first, and then, for a mad-
dening period of months, wind. The movie of *The
Wizard of Oz* had unraveled her, she could not forget the tornado. She hated walking in the streets,
open windows, anything that might let the wind get
to her. Sticky bugs made their appearance about the
time of the eighth anniversary, and at first Amos
thought she meant insects that somehow secreted
some kind of gluey substance, making them hard to
brush off. But gradually, the true fear was revealed
to be anything that stuck you, mosquitoes, bees, black
widows, and Amos, even though he had never finished analysis and his shrink hadn't been a kosher
Freudian, figured the departure of the daddy and the
arrival of the fear had to have some tentacled con-
nection. "No sticky bugs," Amos said. "Can't be."

"Well . . ." She glanced all around the oval. "Why
don't you play and I'll watch first and then later—"

"Honey, don't you read The *New York Times?* In
the first place, it's too early in the year for them, and
besides that, the *Times* printed an article yesterday
about how all the parks had been sprayed against
sticky bugs, so not only can't there be any now, if
they ever try nosing around they're dead, whammo,
just like that. Now come on." He took her hand and
led her. The first thing they came to was the cement
sandbox. He looked at her questioningly.

"Daddy, how can I play in the sand when I'm wearing my spring coat that Mommy boughted for me in Best's? Really."

The teeter-totters came next. "Well?" he asked.

"I'm too light for you. You want to swing me? I'd like that."

There were children's swings with bars to prevent falling out and grown-up swings, and Amos crossed his arms, pointing at both.

"The big," she said, "and I'm the leader." She dashed across the deserted cement and by the time he reached her, she was seated and ready, hands gripping the chains.

Amos began to swing her, carefully, for the swing, one of a row of six, was aluminum, and big enough easily for an adult and he didn't want her slipping. The drunk outside the fence was stirring now, forcing himself up into a sitting position. He had beautiful wavy white hair and a reddish unshaven face and he wore rimless glasses. His clothes were, of course, tatters, but given a decent suit and barber, he could have passed for a business executive easy. Except for the deadly drinking puffs below his eyes. Amos was hoping the guy was bunching his strength for a departure, but no; he just rested sitting, watching them from outside the fence.

"Higher," Jessica called.

Amos pushed a little more as she soared up to his eye level now, her hands locked around the chains, and in her red-and-white-striped coat, she was a lovely thing, because she had her mother's hair, blonde and long, and because his sperm had begun it all. "I'm sorry about the little tiff before," he shouted to her, as she was at the far end of her swing, and each time he returned her there, he called more data: ". . . but I didn't write that show . . . the record, maybe only half of it's mine . . . they fired me . . . I don't write

songs . . . not any more . . . not for four months going
on five now . . . I've never seen that show . . . I never
will . . . okay . . . ?"

"Did Klein know you didn't write the songs?" she
asked, Klein being what Donny insisted she call him.

" . . . he sort of did, see . . . Donny and I had this
kind of scene . . . face to face when I left Philly . . .
we aren't speaking, as they say . . . not to each other
. . . not any more . . ."

"High enough, thank you—I can pump now—" She
began tucking her legs under during the backswing,
kicking forward on the forward move, maintaining
altitude.

Amos went to the swing alongside and sat, watching her sail by.

"That's kind of dum-dum, not writing songs."

"Those ones you sang at the anniversary party were
my first try since they fired me and those weren't my
tunes."

"You're really very silly, Daddy, I have millions of
tunes, you can borrow some."

"I've borrowed from better than you, kiddo."

"Here's one I'm working on," she told him, swinging by, starting to 'la-la' her way through 'On Top of
Old Smoky.' "Like it?"

Amos nodded. "It's got possibilities."

"I'm thinking of calling it 'On Top of Old Smoky'
but that's just a working title."

Amos broke out laughing and started to swing, because he had taught her all the phrases—'working
title,' 'intro,' 'bridge,' 'take it from the top'—and he
loved it when she used them back at him, but it had
been a while since she'd done it. He began to pump,
going little by little higher, adjusting his trench coat
so it wasn't bunched up on the hard sharp-angled
seat of the swing.

"Hey Sam, what rhymes with 'June'?" she called out then, the caption of one of his favorite cartoons, with the two hack song writers huddled helplessly by the piano, and he laughed again, not stopping even when she said, "Write me a song about swinging."

Amos made a smile, shook his head, thinking of even half a year ago when a request like that would immediately bring forth some kind of song, maybe doggerel, but still a song.

She slowed as he pumped higher. "I didn't ask for a *good* song for the heaven's sake, really Daddy, you're just too sensitive."

Amos pumped higher yet. He was going in great arcs now, swooping down, soaring to the front edge of his semi-circle, then floating back again, and for just a moment, there was a fragment of something in there, a couple of notes in some kind of interesting sequence, and he swung higher than ever, staring out beyond the drunk now as the kid stopped swinging and began walking around and wouldn't that be the breathing end, if it all came back to him starting with a kid's request, because, dammit, those notes were nice, they were—they were—

—they were 'Illinois' for chrissakes, that's all. '. . . by thy rivers gently flowing, Illinois, Illinois . . .' That was the sequence he was hearing, part of it anyway, and wasn't that the final laugh, that when you think the dry period is done you end up stealing a piece of junk that you hated in high school and you're so stupid, you're such a dum-dum you think it's interesting *and* original and—the notes inside began changing. The harmonies shifted, and for one second there, Amos thought that maybe there really was going to be a breakthrough, because the second-line tune started like the second-line tune of 'Illinois' but halfway through it broke loose into some-

thing damn near halfway decent but the notes were
dimming on him now and Amos shut his eyes, concentrating on the fading tune as he swung higher and
higher and then he had them maybe, at least he was
hearing something and great art it wasn't and probably they were dull and stank but maybe they were
original, his, and now they were wavering again, tip-
ping off the edge of his mind where you never dared
follow because it was dark down there and Amos
shut his eyes tighter, swung higher, making a grab
and he got there in time, the notes were his if he
wanted them, and he flipped them over and over,
trying to decide, and during the decision came the
bump. He bumped something and he opened his eyes;
he was swinging a little sideways and the world had
turned to stop-time pictures:

He was swinging a little sideways and the kid was
on all fours, facing away, looking for something on
the cement, and the drunk, beyond the fence and facing them both, was having a fit or something, because
he started shouting but who the hell could make sense
of a drunk and

then he was swinging a little less and the kid was
on all fours, and the drunk had staggered off his
bench, heading toward where the fence ended and

now he had stopped swinging but the kid was still
on all fours and the drunk was where the fence
opened, still shouting wildly, pushing his rimless
glasses hard against his nose with one hand, pointing
toward them with the other and

then Amos stood clear of the swing, bracing himself, legs apart, behind the kid, who was still on all
fours, still checking out the cement while the drunk
staggered in on them with the hand that had pushed
the glasses now fumbling into a torn pants pocket
and he was close enough now for Amos to tell that the

other hand, the one still pointing, was unsteady from the booze and

next Amos glanced behind him, to see that nothing could take him by surprise, no other drunk thinking to roll a father and child on a lonely playground, but there was nothing behind to worry about, nothing behind at all, except some red goop on his front swing edge, and as Amos faced front the kid was dripping and the drunk was screaming 'here here' and in his pocket hand he had what must have once been a clean kerchief and Amos thought Jesus, the arrogance of the bastard, he's not asking for dough, he's demanding I put it right in the palm of his hand and

in that instant the bum cried something like 'Jesus' and the kid was spilling now and Amos knew the guy wasn't after loot and as he froze the kid began giving way but

by some miracle Amos knelt and reached her before she reached cement and the drunk stared at the kid, then started to spin, reaching the fence and pitching, spattering some against the bars, and Amos slowly turned his beloved gently over and

at first he thought she was dead, her eyes were rolled up into her head, white only showing where her pupils should have been and

it took a moment before he realized the hole, dime-sized, dime-shaped too, and the amount of blood that flooded through the dime stunned him as it surged across here eyeless face like rapids but without the foam and

Amos brought her to his chest as he stood and spun around, wondering east or west, which way, going "Ohh, ohhh, ohhh" as he turned in the freak afternoon and

"Oh" with each step, "Oh" now shorter, less a moan, more explosive from his lungs, "Oh-oh-oh" as he lugged her east, east was closest, east was best and the drunk was by the fence gate, pitching still as Amos, warmed by the westward-moving sun, kept a steady frantic pace until the child's eyes dropped down unfocused for a moment, until the pain had her, the pain and the fear as she blinked blood and started screaming senseless things until Amos caught *"What have you done to me, Daddy"* and then he lengthened his stride, pressing her poor face against his trench coat, the two of them sopping now and then she lost some consciousness again and

again her eyes went white, and the trees were bare, and the grass was brown, the shadows black, the sky bright blue and through that awful rainbow Amos "Oh"ed his way, clutching his child, the two of them fleeing for his life, unless he was fleeing for theirs, one or the other. . . .

iv

Doctor *Contreras,* for God's sake.

Amos shifted his glance from the child to the ceiling, trying to accept the fact that until some medico named Contreras made an appearance, he was doomed to limbo. Change had never been Amos' buddy, and a life-style shift of this consequence was beyond credence. He smiled down at his daughter, in his arms now as she had been since the happening, and she was rigid, all her wasting strength used in seeing to that, as she clutched her father's holding arms with surprising power, letting Black Amos do his duty, which he did, his remarkable fingers in constant movement, his soft voice a constant companion to her griefs. "Good girl there, Jessica. Yes. I'll say. How I know this must be stingin'. Yes. You just stay like you are. Best I've had. Maybe ever. Yes. What a good girl. What a just fine lady," and on he went, delicately working the offending wound, cleansing the deformity, his slender fingers wrong for his Suma body. A white-clad lady whipped in, threw a hypo into Jessica's arm, took off after. "What was that she gave?" Amos asked.

"Don't know, mister; maybe morphine, maybe Demerol, maybe I don't know 'em all, but she'll feel the better for it. Yes. I'm tellin' you, Jessica, you sure will feel more relaxed. Yes. I promise, you'll feel fine from that. If you want to sleep, you sleep, what a just fine lady."

Amos watched the delicate dark fingers working over his daughter's face, clearing the caked blood,

106

circling the cheek hole over and over. Amos could
study her face now without the least fear of fainting,
which was not so true when he stumbled through the
Borough Hospital's emergency doors ready to shout
for aid, but before he could, it was there, in the odd
black shape of the Suma man who came at them saying "Lemme, lemme, giv'r here," but Jessica started
to panic at that, so Amos simply shook his head and
the Suma man believed and led the way beyond the
waiting room into a small shelter where he drew the
cloth curtain around them and while Amos held on
almost as tightly as Jessica held on, he set to work.
His name too was Amos and you had to figure the
odds were sucker long against something like that
and the white one decided immediately that that was
a symbol sent from Up There meaning don't sweat
it, it's going to be fine. So while Black Amos began
his tidying, and various white-clad people zipped in
with questions and the rest, Amos M. began to actually contemplate the possibility of a happy ending.

Except goddam Contreras couldn't be found.

"You sure this Contreras is good?" Amos asked.

"Doctor Contreras is not only good," came from the
Suma man, "Doctor Contreras is also the only, so
don't you worry about Doctor Contreras, ain't anybody else on."

"You think this can be fixed up okay?" he whispered
indicating his daughter's face.

"Does she come from the planet Crypton? If she
don't, she can be sewn."

"I mean, y'know, so that after . . ." and his gesture,
unseen by the child, made a scar mark along his face.

"Hell, man, I can't see the thing now—Jessica,
which cheek was it got the scratch?—oh yeah I can
make it out now, it was this one here," and he went
back to his soothing preparations. "You know why

it's almost gone, Jessica? On account of you bein' so quiet. I tell you, that's the whole secret to riddin' yourself of these scratches. Quiet. You may just be the quietest in history, so far anyway."

Another white-clad lady hurried in saying, "Doctor Contreras."

Amos whirled on the woman, surprised at his own edge as he took off into "Not here! Actually there is no Doctor Contreras. Doctor Contreras is this great myth—"

"Easy now" from the Suma man.

"You didn't hear me good, mister," the white-clad lady said. "I didn't ask was Doctor Contreras here, I said I was Doctor Contreras."

"Oh," Amos managed. He took a breath, shook his head. "I'm sorry. It's been that kind of day."

Doctor Contreras bent toward Jessica, examining the wound.

Jessica began feebly to kick.

"Don't worry," Amos said. "Daddy's right here." He held the child tighter than ever, and smiled, and studied the doctor, who couldn't have been yet close to thirty-five. She was tiny and all bone and her skin looked stained. She seemed efficient as hell, no doubt, but watching her Amos wondered how he would square it with himself if the operation turned out badly and he had gone and let this practically-in-puberty surgeon lady hack at his kid's face when the last couple of years he had averaged over a quarter of a million dollars per, and there wasn't a stitching specialist in the world he couldn't afford. "Hey?" he said softly. "Could I maybe ask you a couple things?"

"Ask."

Amos nodded to the cloth curtain. "Outside?" She examined the wound in silence a long while longer, then, still silent, she threw back the curtain and stepped beyond. "I'll be just there," Amos said, "right where you can see every sec, so let go, okay?" He released his child, hurried to the doctor, who, clearly impatient, stood solid by the cloth. Amos waved to his daughter, while he whispered "I was just wondering," to Doctor Contreras.

She said nothing.

"I just was interested in how you happened to become a specialist in this kind of thing."

Doctor Contreras said, "What bothers you, mister, that I'm a spic or a broad?"

Amos blinked. "I wasn't being critical, I just—"

"—look, mister—you want to bring down every genius from Massachusetts General, you do that, but the longer we wait, the better the chances she'll scar. You think about that."

"Is she gonna scar?"

"Don't know. Depends."

"No, look, see here's the thing, see the kid and I— I don't want her to scar, Jesus, not on her face, that's not fair—no, look, see the kid and I, we've got this thing going, I mean, we read each other, it's special, and I don't care if every goddam father says what he's got going with his kid is special, what we got going really is and, see, her being here, it's my fault you might say, and—and—"

From Doctor Contreras: "Slow down."

"—and she really is a great kid, you ask anybody, you never came across a better mind, she's quick and she picks up things and she imagines great and you can ask her teachers, I'm not bullshitting you, Doctor, but see, if her face got scarred, well that just can't happen, it wouldn't be right if a thing like that happened because, well, I said I wasn't bullshitting you and I'm not, my kid isn't beautiful, Doctor, and fair is fair, goddamit, it is," and suddenly he reached out, took the small stained lady by the shoulders. "I want you to tell me that you're good. Say you are. Please. That's all."

"I'm good and I'm here. Now do I do the job or do we send the jet for Denton Cooley?"

"You," Amos muttered, hurrying back to Jessica, holding her again. "Didn't I tell you I'd be right back?"

A nurse brought in a rolling stretcher and they transferred Jessica over and then the cloth curtain was thrown back and off they started down the hall, Amos with both hands on the kid till they reached the operating room and he let go for one second because the doorway wasn't quite wide enough for everyone and everything. Then, as he tried to enter, Doctor Contreras was blocking the way.

"Sorry," Amos told her.

"You'll be in the waiting room," Doctor Contreras said.

"Sorry," Amos said, "and don't give me any medical talk about how I'm not sterilized or any other damn thing, I'm not leaving."

"You stay," Doctor Contreras said, "and she'll hate you till she dies."

"Sure," Amos said, not moving.

"*Now you listen, mister*—I'm going to hurt your kid —I'm going to take a needle she'll think is ten feet long and I'm going to jam it *right in that wound*—and I do it slow because it hurts less in the long run but how you going to convey that to a kid? And you don't want to be here when the needle goes in—I'm the doctor—she can hate me all she wants."

"I just think I ought to be here. . . ."

"—the waiting room's plenty close—"

"—don't you do that!" suddenly from Jessica, and Amos turned to see them tying her to the table with sheets, pulling them tight across her small body, knotting them or trying to, because from somewhere she had the strength to really start to kick and cry "Daddy —Daddy don't let them—I'll be good but they're hurting me they are Daddy Daddy I don't wanna be tied—*they're hurting me*—Daddy *I really mean it!*—"

Doctor Contreras closed the operating-room door and Amos allowed it. He stood outside a moment, desperate to hear, but then from inside came the escalating shrieks of the wee one going "Daddy— *Daddy—Daddy!*" mounting toward an animal sound, "*Dah-DEE!—Dah-DEE!—Dah-DEE!*" as most likely the needle entered the tear.

Amos pushed off from the door, floundered a moment, then succeeded in locating the waiting room. He took the chair closest, fell into it, clasped his hands tight together, vised his thighs around them, stared at the floor until the first wave of shakes had subsided. Amos glanced around the room then, noticing it for the first time really. It was a good-sized living room in square footage, with a bunch of metallic chairs set around the perimeter and two extra rows of chairs back to back along the center. There were maybe a dozen people in all present, several of them lined up waiting for the phones: there were two wall jobs with just a curved piece of plastic between them, allowing the speaker no privacy whatsoever. Only one of the phones was working, the other one clearly out of order since it was unused while two people stood impatiently in line for the other. The room was rectangular, blank-walled, metallic, frigid, totally perturbing.

The man across from Amos hiccupped. Then he hiccupped again. "Can't get rid of 'em," he said to Amos.

"Right," Amos said, the 'hic' rhythm already steady

in his brain. In the corner sat a scrawny woman who was having trouble getting air, Amos left her quick enough, then wished he hadn't because the teen-ager three seats down had lost his hands. He had two metal jobs, and they seemed to work okay, since he chain-smoked expertly, making the requisite moves with something close to style. Dazed, Amos realized that the handless one wasn't in need of treatment, it was his companion, a kid brother, clearly, from the facial resemblance, who was painfully holding a hideously swollen thumb, and quickly returning his gaze to his own lap, Amos began wondering what kind of job J. Walter Thompson could do if suddenly faced with the problem of making the room a resort wonderland. 'Put some young in your life with the friendly folk at Borough Hospital—' Amos began to laugh, out loud, always a feepy maneuver, laughing alone, but he kept at it, not minding the stares, really barfing away, even though it wasn't nearly that funny, because in the middle of his ad campaign he remembered Lila and how he had to call her and tell her and she was going to take his head off when she knew. So Amos laughed just as long as he could, and then, dreading every inch of his approach, he stood and started toward the phones. A tiny man was on tiptoe, talking hurriedly and behind him stood a handsome black lady and Amos took his place behind her, staring at the unused phone which had no out-of-order sign.

Standing up, he couldn't reach his kneecaps without putting undue strain on his back, so he took a step out of line to the near wall, began playing tunes with his fingers. The tiny man was still jabbering, in Polish, Amos thought, though he knew not a word of that language. The handsome black lady stood patiently, dime in hand, her hands folded across her

ample bosom. She was perhaps forty-five, Amos
guessed, guessing again that she did domestic work
somewhere for the fancy ladies who lined Fifth and
Madison, flanking the hospital on either side. Amos
played a faster tune against the wall, winging in his
head just how he could best break things to Lila to
forestall the thunderstorm and the best way, if he
could pull it off, was to just play it slow, ease his way
into it.

A Jewish tublike lady moved in behind the black
one then. She glared stolidly at Amos a moment, then
dead ahead at the black neck. Amos, still the step out
of line by the wall, hesitated, then gave his best smile
saying, "I was behind her."

"I said you weren't?"

"No, ma'am, but I just wasn't sure you knew."

"The best way to make sure you got a place in line
is to keep your place in line."

"Yes, ma'am," Amos said, in no mood for battle,
since Lila was looming around the bend and every
ounce of energy was crucial. He smiled again, then
moved away from the wall back directly behind the
black lady. He had expected the tub to retreat one
step, giving him room, but she did no such thing,
standing her ground like Patton, and Amos could feel
her sixty-year-old breasts jabbing him in his back,
not exactly his picture of heaven, but he said nothing
until he became convinced that his testicles were retreating up through his stomach wall, so he half
turned muttering, "Could you maybe give us all a
little room, please?"

She took a while before anything remotely happened. "You never have to go looking for trouble,
you'll learn that, you live long enough." Grudgingly,
she took a half-step backward, giving minimal breathing room.

"No, ma'am," Amos said.

"There's enough trouble in the world without whipping up extra."

"I didn't mean to make trouble. I'm sorry if I did." He faced the black neck again while the Polish man, on tiptoe as before, continued with the phone.

From behind him, Amos heard the tub's voice muttering, "Will he learn."

Amos tried very hard to think about Lila but the muttering kept right on behind him, and Jewish mothers were always hollering 'libel' but where there was smoke, there goddam well was an occasional fire and this one behind him now, pushy and loud and always innocent, would have sent him off the deep end under happy circumstances. Now, it took everything he had to keep Lila on his mind. Ever since his great 'revelation' when he told Lila he was half a Jew there had been certain shifts in his public utterances; he was now free, for example, to shriek his distaste for Miami Beach without charges of bigotry, except that one night he did such a venomous routine against Miami that Lila actually accused him of being a secret anti-Semite—they were in Miami at the time, a year ago, sopping up some February sun but the plastic shoes and mink conventions made him humiliated for his heritage, therefore his blast. The fact that he hated Miami, of course, and swore an oath to her never to return, had nothing to do with any hostility toward his half-race any more than a civilized Irishman's leaving a bar full of loudmouth drunken country-men made him anti-Celt.

From behind him, the muttering was still going on, and Amos, in a final effort to shut her off and maybe win her, gave her his smile again as he turned and gestured idly to the unused phone. "I wonder if it works—" he began.

"—you think I'm so stupid I'd stand here if that one was working?"

"I'm standing here too—I didn't mean anything about being stupid—I just thought, wouldn't it be funny if we were all waiting and right next to us there was a phone and nobody thought to use it."

"To you that's *funny?*"

She moved the half-step in again and with her words now Amos got the terrific smell of onions. He muttered, "Sorry," turned back to the black neck.

"He thinks that's funny," came with onion scent, as the breasts pressed into his back again.

Amos grabbed one of several dimes from his pocket and stepped to the other phone, grabbed the receiver and was about to dial when "You just lost your place in line" hit him hard.

"I was there before you," Amos said.

"Listen—make trouble with somebody else—you left, nobody made you."

Amos was about to shout 'Ten to one your kids are fags' right back at her but instead he jammed his finger into the dialing slots seven times, then, after a moment said, "Lila listen—I'm in this emergency ward but it's nothing serious—we had a little set-to in the park and the kid's with this genius specialist right now—what?—a cut on her face, just a little one but I thought better safe than sorry so I'll call you when the doctor gives me the word. Stay off the phone, huh?" He hung up, headed back toward his chair.

The tub stepped to the empty phone, inserted her dime and, after her second dial, said, "It won't stop buzzing," in the direction Amos had taken.

Amos, back in line behind the black neck, thankful that the Almighty had chosen Now to let him have his tiny triumph, said nothing.

The Jewish lady whirled around facing Amos. "It won't stop buzzing—*all I get is this buzzing.*"

"Listen," Amos answered mildly, "make trouble with somebody else."

"You didn't make any phone call—you were talking to the buzz!"

"There's enough trouble in the world without whipping up extra."

"You expect me to lose my place on accounta this?"

Amos nodded. "You left, nobody made you."

She slammed the receiver back into its cradle. "You think you're some smart guy, don't you?"

"Every so often," Amos agreed.

She grunted her way back behind him while the tiny man said something in his probably Polish tongue, hung up. The handsome black lady moved in and dialed, starting to speak in a singsong Jamaican accent. Amos tried not to listen, but it was all but impossible in the quiet room, and without wanting to, Amos learned that her mother had had a stroke and her son was going to get home by late afternoon and who was going to take care of him? Whoever she was talking to said she couldn't, and the Jamaican lady asked again, a little harder, but there was no change in the answer and the Jamaican lady hung up, hesitated, then took a nearby chair, sitting straight and silent, arms folded as before, across her bosom.

Amos stepped to the phone, and as he began to dial he smelled the onion breath and he wanted to shove the tub the hell away but Lila's number was ringing now so he hunched himself up against the mouthpiece and concentrated on sincerity when he heard Lila's "Yes?"

"Hey, I'm really glad I caught you."

He could sense her stiffening. "Oh?"

"Yeah, I've just been feeling so bad, Lila—about

that little comedy I caused up at your place—you
don't know how sorry I am."

"Oh Amos, I don't believe one word—you loved it
—my God, when was the last time you won anything?"

"Just accept my apology, okay?"

Silence.

The smell of onions.

"I don't know why I misbehaved but see, I've made
a few inquiries now and then about Freddy and all
I hear is these great things about him; I guess I was
jealous, Lila."

A long pause. Then: "Amos? Aren't you at matinee?"

"That's right."

"Then what are you doing on the phone?"

"They've got these new things they're experiment-
ing around with, 'intermissions' they're called, kind of
pauses in the middle, breathing spells. . . ."

Silence.

The smell of onions.

"Let me speak to Jessica, Amos."

"She wanted to hit the ladies' room—"

"—alone?—you let her go alone?—"

"—no—why do you even ask for?—"

"—there's something crazy—I can hear it in your
voice—give me Jessica—"

"—she can't quite come to the phone now—"

"—I want Jessica, Amos—"

"—Lila—"

"—*is she all right?*—"

"of course she's all right, my God, she's fine, just
cool it," and he spun toward the onion smell saying,
"A little room if you don't mind?"

"I'm just holding my place, Mr. Smart Guy, you
talk, I hold."

"Amos who is that?—"

"—the local apparition," Amos answered. "Now about the kid, just listen—"

"Amos, what's happened, you tell me—"

"—nothing's happened, nothing, a little nick, that's all, that's all that's happened I swear, no big deal, I'm sorry I even bothered you about it considering the hysterical—"

"—why can't she talk to me?—"

"—because she's being tended to, obviously; really, Lila—"

"—AMOS, IS SHE HURT?"

"—no, no—"

"—have you hurt her?"

'No,' he was about to say, but the onions were killing him, reeking and foul—

"Amos if you don't answer me I swear to God I'll get you—*tell me damn you, AMOS*—"

"I will," he whispered. "But I can't talk here. I just can't. I swear to God, Lila, it's nothing in the long run and I'll call you in two minutes, just let me get to where there's privacy please," and he found the cradle with the receiver and stumbled toward the swinging door that whirled to the street and on the sidewalk he started toward Fifth, stopped, there weren't any stores on Fifth in the Seventies so he started toward Madison, there were stores on Madison but he stopped again, because Doctor Contreras had said 'You'll be in the waiting room' and what if she came now when he was gone, what if the kid needed him and he was gone, what if the crippling moment in the kid's life came, what if the bone was cracked and they needed his permission to try something fast and he was gone, what, what—

"Dammitshit," Amos shouted, tearing all he had toward Madison because if there was just any place

on the corner with a phone he could belt out his song
to Lila and get back before anyone knew the difference and then he was at Madison but drugstores, no,
stationers, no, nothing but goddam art galleries, every
stinking place you looked art galleries, and the first
one was shut, closed tight, why? because of Lincoln?
never, maybe illness, maybe death but next to the
gallery was a camera place, an open camera place
and Amos said to the woman running things, "Please
I've just got to use your phone" and then he saw the
phone, down a ways and she didn't tell him yes, even
when he dropped a quarter on the counter as he
made his way toward it, instead she answered, her
voice Teutonic, the accent thick, "Votch oud for mine
puppy" and Amos glanced back at her, then screamed,
as up from the ground leapt a giant shepherd, bark-
ing and growling and going for him with white teeth
and yellow eyes and Amos fell back but the beast
kept coming and the Nazi lady said, "Votch oud I
told you" and Amos brought his arms up to protect
his face from the monster until he realized that a
rope held it, a rope of decent thickness but the thing
must have weighed close to a hundred and the rope
was already frayed and Amos heard "He don't hardly
get oud never" but that wasn't enough reassurance
for him, not nearly enough, because the thing was a
killer dog and there wasn't any way he could match
it, so panicked he fled back to the Madison corner,
where he froze, gaping around for a phone because
he had been gone too long already if Contreras
needed him but he couldn't move, he simply could
not move until it happened, from behind him, the cry
of "no—no" in a terrible German accent and the dog
was loose, the dog was free, and it was on the sidewalk, half a dozen feet of frayed rope dangling from
its collar and Amos took off silently, back for the hos-

pital, praying to sweet God the dog didn't see him
and the hospital was up ahead too far, too fucking
far, because behind him now there was that deadly
growl and he knew it was after him and he looked
back dreading the sight of the yellow-eyed thing eating up the ground and Amos ducked his head and
pumped his arms because he had a chance, a long
one but he could make it with every break in all the
world and then to his horror the Emergency door
opened and there was Contreras with the kid in her
arms, as she left the safety of the revolving door, her
face freezing as she saw what was coming toward
her and Amos glanced behind again and now Contreras screamed and the shepherd veered toward the
sound and Christ, Amos thought, the fucking thing's
going after the kid and he couldn't have that, no matter what, he could not face the next dawn if that
happened and as the beast cut toward Contreras
Amos blindly dove and hit the thing in the side and
they tangled terribly, and Amos cried out as the thing
bit his hand, his right hand, the rough teeth entering
his flesh and he had never experienced pain before,
not retching pain, and he almost threw in the towel
right then except he couldn't, not with his left still
working, and from somewhere, maybe childhood he
remembered that if you ever had to stop a dogfight
you had to wade in and grab the nearest beast by
the testicles and it had to be from childhood, because
the word 'testicle' had stunned him then but he flung
his left toward the shepherd's under-belly and down
and the thing was deeper into his right hand now and
Amos was afraid he would pass out before he could
do it but he didn't as his left hand closed with every
ounce of what passed for strength he had around the
shepherd's testicles and Amos yanked, God Amos
yanked, and the beast screamed and let go of the

ruined hand and to his horror Amos felt his own grip
giving, and the dog kicked so violently as to fall over
hard to the street, but free again and Amos made it
to his knees before the charge and the thing came
for his throat where his right arm was positioned, and
the arm deflected the charge but not before its force
knocked Amos back into a post and the air started
going out of him as the thing came again and Amos
did his best to turn and take the brunt on his shoulders but he forgot his unprotected neck and the thing
sunk its teeth there, the nerve-filled neck, but not a
good grip, the bite was superficial, and as Amos completed his turn his left hand closed around the rope
and the rope closed around the neck of the beast and
then the thrashing began, the sounds unendurable
and Amos could feel his strength going but he knew
that if he let go, it was over, over and done but thank
Jesus at least the kid was back inside and safe and
fuck it, it didn't matter about him, he was used up
anyway, and the beast kicked and screamed and Amos
only held onto the rope as it cut the breath away and
probably there wasn't any scar so Lila didn't have to
get so excited, probably there was just one of those
childhood happenings that never leaves a memory
and later you wonder what you had gotten so excited
about except there wasn't going to be a later for him,
not unless he hung on but he couldn't do that, all his
power was gone now and the stench was nauseating,
as the dog defecated all over the street, its dead mus-
cles relaxing, and as the excrement poured out, Amos
released the rope, and as the stench grew he could
feel his grip on reality going and all he wanted was
for his hand by some miracle to be made whole again
and to rest, but the German lady was not to allow
that because, dazed and drifting, Amos seemed to
hear her screaming at him, vilifying him, raining him

with curses for his cruelty and then she was with a
blue man, and Amos couldn't make out anything any
more, and was the guy a regular cop or someone from
the hospital, there was just no way of telling, he was
blue and he was authority and Amos was defenseless.
"Look vut he dit to my puppy—five hundred dollars
and look vut happens—" ". . . lady . . . I didn't . . ."
but the effort was too much and she was screaming
now, "*See? See vut he did?*" and Amos was aware of
forms now as a crowd began to gather and the tub
from the emergency-room telephone was behind the
German lady now and the tub was going, "You look
for trouble, you find trouble, you look for trouble,
trouble's what you find," and then, thank God, came
Contreras. She launched into the German lady: "That
rotten dog of yours has scared the crap out of every
kid around here since I started interning, so forget
that puppy line, all right?" She glanced at the blue
man. "Get everybody moving, Fred," and he answered, "Whatever you say, Doctor Contreras," and
then he faded as Contreras whirled on the tub from
Emergency with more vehemence than Amos had
encountered from her. "I'll put you in jail, I swear to
God." "I didn't do nothing but stand here," the tub
began but Contreras wasn't having any—"I'm telling
you and you better hear me good: don't you set foot
in that Emergency waiting room again, you sadistic
bitch, you got no business there, you just like to wal-
low in other people's pain, now I see you near that
emergency ward one more time I'm swearing out a
warrant." She called out to the policeman then: "Fred,
get these people outta here, all of 'em, now!" She
dropped beside Amos, reached for his ruined right
hand and the sudden anguish was so intense he had
to crack wise or cry. ". . . Will I be able to play the
violin when my hand heals . . ."

"This?" Contreras studied his fingers. "This is nothing. Of course you will."

"Good," Amos managed. "I never knew how before." He tried to laugh.

"Make all the bad jokes you want, you're entitled, you're a brave man."

"Always on Wednesdays," Amos replied, another joke, worse than the first, but he needed cover, you couldn't let a toughie like Contreras embarrass you. Because he wasn't brave, not remotely. Anything but, really, since you couldn't call brave a man who was frightened by roaches and water bugs and being alone. What else, Amos wondered. I'm afraid of anything that slithers or stings and my ex-wife, who does both. And I'm afraid of the dark and I'm afraid of falling and getting trapped in an elevator and I'm afraid of crazy people and being alone, no, I already counted that. But Contreras was no bull artist and whatever the reasons, I did do it, no matter what, however bad the kid's face ends up, I took a risk for someone else, I'm a coward who maybe once was brave, I'm Amos McCracken and I don't write songs and my ex-wife hates me and my death won't bring forth much mourning but screw that, who cares about that, 'cause it's down in the record books and there it's gonna stay: I'm Amos McCracken and I fought the fucking dog.

"Let's get you into Emergency," Contreras said, waving Black Amos close. He was holding the kid, so she relieved him of that burden. "Your daughter's out of things for a while, so don't worry that her eyes are closed, okay?"

Amos could feel himself being lifted as he stared at his daughter.

"Well?" Contreras said, holding the kid close for Amos to see.

"There's no scar," Amos said. "Where's the scar—there's no scar. . . ."

"I told you I was good," Contreras said. They were moving in a group toward the emergency door. She smiled for the first time then. "Lucky. It happens sometimes. A clean wound, no broken bones; it happens."

Amos could not take his eyes from his daughter's face. "She's so beautiful."

"I told you; lucky."

"No," Amos said. "I mean she doesn't—what the hell's different—you did something—she always had great blonde hair but the rest—you're gonna laugh but she doesn't look like Bert Lahr any more."

The revolving Emergency door was just ahead of them now. Contreras smiled again, and now she was embarrassed. "It was nothing," she answered. "But the wound closed so well I tried a skin thing, never mind the technical bull, you tighten the skin's what it comes down to and I only did it because while I was closing the wound I thought if it wasn't for the way her face wrinkled, she could be such a stunning kid, don't laugh but she reminded me of Carole Lombard, and I think it came out all right but don't think I'm saying she'll always look like Lombard, faces change, who the hell knows."

The revolving door turned and Amos was back in Emergency, his mind filled with Carole Lombard, stunning and blonde and warm and he said, "Has Doctor Contreras been around?" to the girl at Emergency Reception.

"She's still operating," the girl answered.

Amos nodded to her and sat back down in the chair he had first tried fifteen minutes before, across from the hiccupping man. The Jewish tub was still using the phone, but there was no one in line behind her.

His fingers working overtime on his kneecaps, Amos waited. Whoever had architected the room had been genuinely sadistic about the phone placement, since most of what the tub was saying was audible everywhere, she was a loud talker, but still, it seemed like the kind of room that even if you whispered, anyone on the perimeter would gather your meaning. Now, for example, along with the rhythmic 'hic . . .' he could tell the tub was talking to her sister, that gallstones were somehow involved, and dinner was out of the question. As the call ended, Amos was out of his seat, only to reclaim it as the tub produced two nickels and dialed again. It was another sister this time, and clearly they were not on the friendliest of terms, which worked in Amos' favor because the call was quick. Again the tub hung up. Amos waited. The tub hesitated, sighed, moved to a chair across the room.

Amos got to the phone fast, fumbled his dime into the slot. The fact that there was no one waiting behind him this time relieved some of the pressure, if only Lila was maneuverable, but she had this terrible tendency to hysteria on occasion, and there was no coping with her then. Amos completed the dial and before the first ring fully ended she was on him—"Why so long?"

He could hear it right off, the controlled frenzy, so he used the only gambit that ever even sometimes paid, a lulling monotone, rambling and steady. "Now honey, it hasn't been that long, I tried getting to a private phone and this dog, you should have seen it, Lila, if they remake *The Hound of the Baskervilles* that one has got to be the star, and it scared the bejesus out of me, so I came back where I started, and I haven't got any too much privacy, so I'll try taking it nice and easy, why don't you try? It's just been a couple of minutes, that's all, look at your watch, baby, you'll see, I'm right, just take a look and tell me if it's been all that long."

"Who's tending to her, Amos? You said she couldn't talk to me because she was being tended to."

It was working; her voice was down some already. "I did say that, that's right. A genius specialist is giving her the once-over this very minute."

"Yes, go on, Amos."

"Nothing to go on about, baby."

"Please. Go on, Amos."

"Well, we were in the park and there were some swings and—"

"—and you pushed her too high and she fell."

"Do you want to hear or don't you?"

"I'm sorry. Go on, Amos."

"We were on the grown-up swings and she was swinging. I got her started nice, and then I took a few spins on the one alongside and she got down, I guess, and tripped and my swing grazed her cheek and I knew what a demon you were about infections so I got this genius specialist—"

"—I don't understand 'infections.' You mean it broke the skin and you were worried?"

"Well of course, Lila, what else would I mean?"

"Go on, Amos."

"You know as much as I do."

"You said 'I guess' she tripped. I don't understand— weren't you right there?"

"Of course I was right—"

"—then why do you have to guess, couldn't you just see what happened?"

"My eyes were closed at the time."

"Oh. Now I get it. You were swinging and she tripped and the swing grazed her face and it cut the skin so you thought a doctor ought to take a peek."

"A plus."

"I don't believe you, Amos."

Amos closed his eyes as the smell of onions hit him again. "I know you don't."

"Go on, Amos."

"In essence—" Amos began.

"—don't give me any 'essence' shit—"

"—Lila, I can't talk loud, so please—" and he turned, staring at the tub who was half a step away. "I really would like some privacy."

"I have to use the phone," the tub answered.

"You can use it when I'm done."

"That's my plan, Mr. Troublemaker."

"You don't have to stay right on top of me, dammit."

"—Amos—"

"My husband just passed a gallstone, mister, and I only wish it should be you sometime so you could know a little what it's like, suffering, pain, and I hafta use the phone. I got sisters to call, I got in-laws to call, and I don't budge."

"Lila," Amos whispered, "listen—"

"Is she permanently scarred?" Lila said, her voice so soft and surprising that Amos, before he knew it, answered, "Maybe, depends, I don't know, they don't know, nobody knows."

Amos could hear Lila breathing.

"I didn't mean it, I was swinging, and daydreaming, I guess, and the swing must have caught the kid on the cheek, that's what must have happened," The onion smell crawled across his skin.

"Well," Lila said. "That just goes to show you should listen to people."

Her voice was soft again, and Amos, braced for shrieks, was grateful, even though he didn't understand what she was talking about. "We both should, Lila," he replied, scrambling for safety.

"You're just not capable and you never have been but it doesn't matter any more."

"Oh come on, what are you talking about, I'm not all that bad, Lila, you're—"

"—it doesn't matter what you are, Amos; it's over."

"Five cents for the next five minutes please."

Amos rummaged in his change pocket. "I've only got dimes and quarters."

"You will have to put in five cents for the next five minutes."

"If I put in a quarter will I get extra time?"

"Five cents for the next five minutes or this call will be disconnected."

Amos shoved a quarter into the largest slot, heard the 'chung,' was about to begin when Lila edged him out with, "You're done, Amos."

"Done?"

"That's right. With Jessica."

"Lila—"

"If I'd only just listened to people—but I was stubborn—Freddy told me to stop it—letting you see Jessica."

"Freddy. You mean that great father figure Frederick A. Hunter that gives you your jollies these days?"

"Everybody says it. *You're dangerous, Amos.* You're this inept mass that somehow makes it through the day, but you're dangerous to anyone around you."

"What do you mean you won't let me see the kid?— quit talking crazy, Lila—"

"—I will not expose that child to you, not any more—"

"—you can't stop me from seeing the kid—there's the law—"

"—that's right, Amos." Singsong.

"I'm the father, so you wipe that goddam ugly thought off your goddam ugly mind, nothing's gonna stop me."

"You can stop you."

"Huh?"

"We'll go to court over it—I may lose—*but if I do I'll lose in court*—the papers will pick it up; after all, you're quite a famous fella, you wrote *Francie*, the *Daily News* will eat you with a spoon."

"There's no dealing with you when you get hysterical."

"I'm not hysterical, Amos."

It was true. It was true. He was hearing only hatred, pure, not simple. Amos pushed his lips against the mouthpiece, whispering, "It would just get all so ugly, don't even make a threat like that, please."

"I'll put the kid on the stand, Amos."

"You think you're gonna panic me with your stupid threats—"

"No threats, Amos. Statements of fact—now where are you? I'll come and take over."

"This was just a freak thing today, I swear, a billion-to-one long shot, so don't even pretend about going to court or anything, please, Lila—"

"—how badly is she hurt, Amos?—"

"I told you, I don't know, maybe badly maybe not, now don't go on about any court business, we got to think of the kid."

"That's all I am thinking of, Amos, and right now I-cannot-conceive-of-a-single-action-in-this-world-I-would-not-commit-to-keep-her-safe-from-you! I'm much stronger than you are, Amos. I can face the courts. I can put her on the stand. What can you do?"

"I really need to keep seeing the kid, Lila—"

"Where are you?"

"I won't tell unless you promise you were only kidding—but I will cut down some on the visits—how's that?—that's fair—it really is, Lila—on my word of honor I'll cut down some, you can't ask for more than that."

"Tell me where you are."

"Didn't you hear me?" Amos shouted it with everything he had. "I won't tell where we are until you tell you were kidding, then I'll tell, but you've got to say you didn't mean it, *I need the kid, Lila.*"

"You want me to say I didn't mean it? Sweet Jesus—" her voice was going up. *"You son of a bitch you scarred my baby, where are you?"*

"Call you when the doctor's done," he said, pushing the phone away, hanging up quickly before she forced the answer from him. He took the first seat he came to and tried to figure just how bad his pickle was, how deep the pit, how slick, how hard to climb?

Well, you couldn't really exult about the way things were going. But then, of course, like they say, things could always be a lot worse, etc., only Amos couldn't quite make out how. And he couldn't catch the afternoon; it was going by, he knew that. He could see the outside air darkening as it does in February, but he couldn't grab onto anything substantial, he just sat there weightless and free-associating and every so often Lila would flash on in living color, green eyes deadly. Once they had worshipped him, those eyes, and maybe if he had gotten icky with emotion and blabbed his undying, etc., she wouldn't be taking the kid away from him now. It was like borrowing from banks when you don't need to, when you do pay it back you're building up this reservoir of good will and credit and you can call on it in crisis and God knows he was making his home there now, in crisis, a suburb of trauma, on the outskirts of anguish, by the shore of lake loathing, in the county of pain.

Contreras was looking at him.

Amos looked back up at her, blinking.

"Let's get you some coffee," from Contreras.

"Is she scarred?"

Contreras led him into the Emergency Ward and through it to a small cafeteria. "Of course she's scarred—I just sewed her face back up. What you mean is will she be scarred permanently."

"Will she be?"

"There's bound to be a mark," Contreras said. "How do you take it, black?" She indicated the coffee machine.

Amos made a nod, sitting at a table in the corner of the small bright room while she came back with two cups and sat across from him.

"A bad mark?"

"I'll tell you in two years. It'll take that long at least to be sure. But I don't think so."

"How many stitches?"

Contreras shook her dark head. "You work from the inside out. There's all those layers, forget the medical jargon, but there's muscle and bone covering and fat and you close them up as you go along. Layer by layer you stitch it shut, but you don't count."

"How about the pain?"

"They put themselves out. That's why I had to make

you leave. They can't distinguish between touch and pain. Everything that comes close to them might be pain and so they react to it that way until you've got it deadened. Then the eyes roll back in the heads sometimes—I think it's self-hypnosis—they go somewhere you can't hurt them. When it's all over, they snap to and burble on and then they get tired and drop off and then they're awake again and blabbering like there was no tomorrow. When you go see her, don't be surprised, I got a big pressure bandage over almost half her face. To keep everything where it should be for a few days."

"But it'll go away, the scar?"

"By third grade you probably won't see it. Drink your coffee."

"I don't want my coffee."

She shrugged, drank hers.

"She looks bad, huh, with that bandage thing and all?"

"No worse than you right now."

"What I mean is, her mother's gonna take it bad, the kid, the way she looks and all?"

Contreras shrugged again. "Depends on the mother." She finished her coffee, started to stand. "Come on, I'll let you see for yourself."

Amos couldn't help laughing.

"You want to lie down?" Contreras said.

Amos managed a shake. "It's just—" he started, then stopped till the laughter subsided—"I know you must think I'm manic and all, but sometimes, when you're big stupid, you just have to laugh at yourself, you do, I swear to God. After all, here I am, coming on with all these dopey things like how many stitches and how's her mother going to feel, and I almost forgot the one really crucial question."

"What's that?"

"Can she travel?"

V

Dante opened the door, scowled prettily, exited deep into the apartment.

Amos moved to the living room carrying the kid, who seemed almost unalive. He knelt, gently depositing her on the couch, doing his best to shape her into a comfortable position. He unbuttoned her red-and-white-striped coat and examined her battered face to see if anything was going wrong, any blood suddenly bubbling out from the bandage edges, but there was nothing. He was opening his trench coat, the blood-stained front dry now, when Donny bounced into the room. "As I live and breathe," Donny began, "or has somebody said that already."

"I was just in the area," Amos began, "I thought I'd stop by."

Then neither of them said much for a moment. The room they stood in was filled with bric-a-brac, most of it old, all of it valuable. The building, in the sixties on Central Park West, was large and dark and peopled with ladies like the room, most of them old, all of them valuable. Donny began to tidy and fluff and plump until he saw Jessica.

"Dear God," escaped him, and it sounded sincere in spite of the fact that Donny didn't like children.

"Little accident, she'll be fine."

Donny stared down at the still child. "She's not going to expire suddenly or anything like that?"

"She won't bleed on your cushions, you can relax."

Donny began circling the dark room again. Beyond the windows, the West Side was growing particularly gloomy as dusk hit it. "I'm having company, Amos, I'm in the midst of mad preparations, and I must tell you I am thoroughly confused. You call—out of the blue, or has somebody said that already?—for the first time since our Philadelphia curtain scene you phone up and I say I'm busy and you say you don't care, you've got to see me—well, now you've seen me, Amos; I really must get back to my kitchen duties."

"You don't cook, Donny. Why didn't you pick a better excuse?"

"Because I wanted you to know I was lying, *bubby*."

Jessica made a sound then, not a pain sound, just an intake, and Amos went to his knees beside the couch, stroking her pretty hair. "Dante's not in the show any more, I guess."

Donny, across the room, swacked cushions. "It was too dreary—the thing's dying on cut-rate tickets now and there wasn't much point in exposing him to that. Actually, the stage isn't his prime medium; his future lies in films."

"Doing any writing or anything?" Amos asked.

"You can stall all you want before getting to it, Amos, it's fine with me—just so you understand this: *I'll do anything in the world for you except a favor.* Clear? Now, as a matter of fact, I'm dabbling with a film script—the theatre seems terribly sterile to me just now, doesn't it to you?"

"Donny, listen . . ."

"—no—"

"—you don't even know what I'm going to ask for—"

"—No!—"

"Jesus—"

"—remember Philadelphia?—when you came to

my room all packed and ready to go and looking for blood, do you recall?"

"I was upset. I'd just been canned for no reason and—"

"You'd gone dry, Amos! It was simply business! I would have been canned too if it had come to that and you'd have pushed me toward the nearest passing train."

"*Donny I need some help.*"

"*Shit some!*"

"What did I do to you that was so terrible in Philadelphia?—for chrissakes I went dry trying to write a song for Dante, our great male ingenue lead—I never wanted to write the goddam song but you said do it! and I tried, didn't I try? and the night I'm banished and leaving I stop by and there you are with him and the two of you are bombed out of your skulls and acting so cutesy I wanted to toss my cookies and all of a sudden it hits me that all those days I'm upstairs busting my balls for our no-talent stinking ingenue you're downstairs fucking him—*I didn't even know you were queer, Donny.*"

"Your naïveté cannot be blamed on me."

"I thought we were friends."

"Your naïveté cannot be blamed on me."

Jessica made another sound, and Amos shifted her slightly, straightening her, comforting her as best he could.

"You said bad things about me, *bubby;* squalid things, unforgivable things. But it wasn't the name-calling—I've been called worse by lovers—I couldn't take the face that went with it—why do you think I paraded and camped if it wasn't so you'd know?— you were in trouble and I wanted you to understand I had troubles too—I'm fifty-two years old and my heart's gone to a dumb dago but he's twenty-eight

and beautiful and how could I get him and keep him
and keep any dignity, I can't, and I want my *bubby*
to see why I've been such a shit to him—*I was out
of control*, Amos, so I let you in on my little secret
and my God, why do you think I'm doing this dreadful screenplay, if it sells I'll lose him if it doesn't sell
I'll lose him and you shouldn't have looked at me the
way you did that night, Amos, I thought *we* were
friends and I said let's have a drink and you said no
and I said dear God *Please* and you said No!, well,
that's what I'm saying now, *No!*, because I am not and
never was the black vomit you made me feel when
you looked at me that night when I needed help from
you but none was forthcoming and I really must
get back to my kitchen chores, *bubby*, you'll just have
to excuse me."

Amos buttoned his coat, hers, folded her up into
his arms. "I was just in the area," he said, "I thought
I'd stop by," and then he was out in the street, and
it was raining. No. It wasn't raining, it just should
have been raining, he was being anthropomorphic, or
maybe that wasn't the word, but in fairy tales they
were always telling you how the forest felt sad and
it really didn't it was only trees, and it wasn't really
raining now, he was just being onomatopoetic or al-
literative or maybe empathy was the word he was
after, and wouldn't a teaspoonful of that taste be just
the thing to set the old blood coursing along about
now?

An empty cab cruised by and Amos grabbed it,
carefully getting in backward, holding the kid against
his blood-stained trench coat, protecting that cheek
as best he could until they were safely on the seat.
Then he closed the door gently. He glanced at his
watch, saw it had already turned five so he gave the
West Forty-eighth Street address even though he

hadn't called to see if anyone was there; he had to take the chance. The cab cut over toward Lincoln Center, then down to what would eventually turn into Ninth, as Amos glanced out at the darkness, then down at the battered head beside him. Her eyes began to open so he bent close. "Hi sleepyhead."

After a beat she said, ". . . hi . . ."

"Bet you're feeling better."

After a beat she said, ". . . fine . . ."

"You've got a lot more color."

Finally, she nodded.

He studied her carefully—she had done this twice before already since they'd left the hospital, come to, but slowly, then picked up like Whirlaway hitting the home-stretch, then just as suddenly unwinding again, the energy gone. He waited for her to begin to make her move. She didn't, so he did what he could to get her motor turning. "Sun in your eyes?" he said.

". . . there isn't any sun . . . how can there be sun when it's dark? Oh I see, you were teasing."

"Guilty," right hand high.

". . . really, Daddy, you're always doing that, just tease, tease, tease, every time you turn around."

Amos nodded. "I'm terrible."

"Oh, no, you're not terrible, you're a terrible *tease* but you're not terrible."

"No I'm not," Amos said. "Actually, adorable is what I am."

She shook her head.

"You just don't know, miss, because while you were snoozing away here I was just announced as winner of this year's Sandra Dee Award, Contestants are judged on poise, personality and musical talent competitions and I was the leader."

She was really revved up now, almost giggling, but then her head was giving her trouble and there was, briefly, pain across her face and then, almost like a finger snap, she was back to being unalive.

Amos sat there, stroking her hair. This had been the briefest conscious period, and what did that mean? Nothing. Nothing to worry about anyway. She's been through a lot and she was tired and when you were tired you slept, period. Amos examined the bandage again for blood seepage but there wasn't a speck and Contreras would have said if anything damaging might happen so *quit worrying about it*.

Worry about the scene coming up on Forty-eighth Street if you want to worry about something.

When they got there, the cab glided slowly between Ninth and Tenth Avenues. In the darkness, Amos wasn't exactly certain which the building was, so once he was in the right vicinity he paid, got out, again with great care, and as the cab pulled off, he clutched the wee one to him and did what he could to stifle his fears. It was such a treacherous slum, why in the name of God would anybody live here if they didn't have to? Amos looked at his watch. Five-fifteen. The street seemed nothing but shadows, and they frightened him—it had been a freaky day from the crazy heat on down, and even more things than usual frightened him now as he stood there in the darkness waiting. A derelict moved by, striving for sobriety. A mean wind started kicking up, and Amos did what he could to shield the battered face with his body, shifting her from one position to another, his arms aching. The kid moaned. Amos shivered. Then the wait was over.

"Betsy!"

"Amos . . . ?"

He raised his right hand. "Guilty."

"Good God what happened?" Betsy reached out,

carefully stroked Jessica's hair away from where it had tumbled over the pressure bandage.

"She had an argument with a swing and lost— listen, I was kind of hoping you'd come home after the matinee, are you busy or anything?"

He followed her as she unlocked her way into her ground-floor apartment. The place was even sadder than her smile, a tiny living-room/bedroom combo, peeling and postered, a kind of kitchen hidden behind a curtain along one wall. The place seemed unchanged since his last visit, around Christmas, the night Lila had taken off for the Mexican divorce, when he'd come calling unannounced, the antique gold bracelet in his pocket. He'd bought it originally for Lila, to commemorate their eighth, but they'd separated before he'd handed it over. Amos hadn't seen Betsy since their little fling in Philly, and once she'd taken him inside, he gave her the band of antique gold. It cost eleven hundred and change, so it was hard to be casual, but he did what he could, going, "Listen, I just happened to see this and I thought you might like it."

She just stared at the thing. "Oh Amos," she managed then, "you didn't just happen to think I might like this."

"I didn't?" he said quickly.

"You're such a liar—you bought this for me because Lila's gone and you were afraid I might throw you out, isn't that more like it?"

"Closer, maybe," he admitted truthfully. It was a little closer.

"You've got a rotten opinion of yourself; you don't have to buy me. Hell, I've slept with lots worse guys than you." Amos laughed and Betsy put the bracelet tenderly on and then she started to ramble and it soon came clear that Amos, without knowing or want-

ing, had touched some secret place along the thin
edge of her psyche; she was moved, not by the gift's
cost, which she never knew, but by his need of it.
She was always collecting strays and that he had gone
to all the trouble of buying her the bracelet simply
to assure acceptance proved only what a bottomless
view he had of himself and to rid him of that, for one
of her limited capabilities, well, would she ever be
equal to the task . . . ?

Amos put the kid on Betsy's bed, examined the
pressure bandage, saw all was well, glanced at Sweet
Betsy, the gold bracelet as ever on her left wrist. It
was twenty after five by his trusty chronometer, and
he started to speak and was aware of how much faster
than usual the words were tumbling out, but there
wasn't much he could do about it. "Listen, I'm in
this kind of plight, you might put it, a bit of a mess,
and because of certain prevailing conditions there
aren't all that many I can turn to but you're one, so
give me your word you won't let me down, okay?"

She stared down at the dazed child. "Should she
be out like this? Amos, we only broke up this morning, what the hell's going on?"

"Like I told you, a swivet, a strait, can I handle
words or can I handle words, and you'll help old
Amos, right, keed?"

"She's awful pale, shouldn't she be at a doctor?"

"Quit answering me with questions, just say yes!"

"Well, you're acting funny."

"If I'm acting funny, it's because you're costing me
time, Betsy, and I'm fresh out, see, it's five-twenty-two
and ticking."

"I've got a little Scotch," Betsy said. She found the
bottle by the sink, poured some into a glass, poured
some more for herself.

"If you want proof," Amos began, swallowing the

Scotch, "proof is that I just paid my first visit to Donny and it didn't go too good but you've got to know I'm serious if I'd try for help from him."

The kid breathed.

Amos dropped to her, whispering, "Oh baby, just hang in there, take it nice and easy, it's gonna be fine, it is, yes."

Betsy, above them, asked, "What's this about?" and Amos whirled on her, rising.

"Possession!—that's the gist of it, you want to know, possession, and you know what possession is, it's nine-tenths and I am right now the possessor and that is the way things are going to be until *I* say otherwise, and Lila wants to be the possessor but I can't have that, not in this world thank you, so for the first time in months I'm using the old noodle, Betsy my girl, I've got plans that will startle the civilized world, but in order to expedite them, in order to really get them greased and flowing, there's this little commodity I'm shy on, cash."

"I haven't got any money, Amos. Maybe twenty-five dollars, I'll let you have twenty if that's any help."

"It's a beginning, let's be charitable and call it that." He sat by the child and began brilliantly drumming his fingers on his knees. "See this basic situation contains an irony, namely that here I am, with thousands coming in each week but the banks are closed and you've got to give your name to loan companies and credit cards are traceable and in my pocket this very moment is a traveler's check for fifty and close to sixty in cash, totaling a hundred ten, and with your twenty I'm a hundred thirty but I figure the magic number to get me through the night is two five oh so I'm barely more than halfway home. Can I have yours?" He pointed to her glass.

She hmanded it to him, he downed it, then reached

into his wallet, got a blank check, began filling it out. "Now hear me, Betsy, this is kind of crucial; tomorrow, you are going to take this little check of mine to the Chase Manhattan Bankerino at East End Avenue at Eighty-third Street, together with a little note I'm going to write out for you next, and you're going to give it to a Mr. John Gilroy, who is an old and dedicated employee, and then he is going to hit you with a fat twenty-five hundred bucks which you will then get to me in a method I'm about to specify—"

"—Amos, is all this legal, whatever it is?"

"Obviously, cherub."

"Then why don't you get it?"

"That's my genius concept, the gasper, the stunner, the one that leaves them all lapping your wake because here's Lila, see, all the trump cards in her manicured paws, right? And she says, *she* says I'm not capable and no more wee one for me, only she's got this one little niggling minor roadblock, which is lack of possession and so the reason I can't get the money myself tomorrow morning Sweet Betsy is mainly a geographical one, I ain't gonna be here."

Betsy waited.

Amos rolled on. "And she'll never guess where I'm going 'cause it's where I'm safe and sound, the last place she'd ever come up, she'd be old and full of sleep before she ever got it figured, I'm taking the wee one to Miami, Sweet Betsy, I'm flying her out tonight."

"Christ, Amos, that's kidnapping—"

"Funny?—Funny? How can it be kidnapping when the napping kid is mine?—can I use words or can I use words? My baby had an accident, Betsy, and I'm getting her down to some sunshine, that's the extent of my actions, and you, with your *True Confessions* mind, call it kidnapping." He went for the Scotch bottle, emptied it into his glass. "Now Lila has conceivably called out the local law by now, which is why I had to go to Donny and you, people she'd never think of calling or doesn't know about, where's your Yellow Pages?" She pointed under the bed and he yanked it out, flipped through, dialed. In a moment he was speaking. "Listen," Amos began, "I've got kind of a good chronometer I bought a couple years ago in Rome and you people do that sort of thing, don't you, let people have money for things and like that, I've never done this exactly before."

"You'll have to bring it in, I can't quote prices without first seeing the merchandise."

"Great," Amos said. "Listen, you're on Eighth Avenue between Forty-first and Forty-second?"

"That's right."

"Well I'll be on down."

"We close at six."

Six? Jesus it's almost that now, who stays open later?"

"State law, we have to close at six, we open in the morning at—"

"—morning's no good, I'll be there, just wait *please*," and he hung up. He hesitated a moment, then, before saying it: "Betsy, let me have that gold bracelet back, okay?"

"I'm not going to get involved in this, Amos—"

"—I have no *time*—doncha see, you'll airmail special me the twenty-five hundred but I gotta survive till then on cash, no credit cards, no loans, no nothing Lila can trace me with, and the kid and I, we can cut it easy down there for a while on twenty-five hundred and when it's gone, *then* I'll call Lila and *then* we'll see if maybe she doesn't find me a little more capable and *then*, once she's said yes, the kid's mine as much

as I want, back we come, but I gotta be invisible a
while, Betsy, so just give me the bracelet, huh?"

"—it's kidnapping and I'm not getting involved!"

"Be a little bright for me once—I need two hundred and fifty, just to be on the safe side, for taxis
and plane fare and I've got to feed the kid and buy
her stuff to keep her happy till your envelope with
the twenty-five hundred arrives—I'll call you from
Miami—we'll hole up in some motel and I'll phone
you the address and then once the envelope comes,
we'll go someplace really swell, on the ocean, first
class, the sun's going to do wonders for the kid, she's
had kind of a tough day."

"I won't send you the money, Amos. I mean that.
I'm not getting involved."

"The bracelet, Bets."

"*Amos, no.*"

"You are involved right as of now, don't you know
anything?"

"—I am not—"

"—you're not, huh, well hear this, oh mistress mine,
I'm pawning this watch and the shops are closing
and in order to get there, I'm gonna hafta *move* and
if you're not involved I'm gonna hafta take the kid
with me and you know what that's gonna do to her
cheek—the running and the bouncing, it could split
it wide open and you know that's true and I'd like to
leave her here while I get the pawning done."

She looked whipped, so there was no surprise when
she said, "All right, you can leave Jessica here, I'll do
that much."

"*Then you're involved!* What's the difference how
much, any penetration is sodomy and any help makes
you an accomplice, so give me the bracelet, it's all
part of the same thing, because I can get a couple of

hundred easy for the bracelet and that puts me over the top."

Betsy hesitated.

"It was never yours—I bought it for Lila for our eighth—it was always hers, always meant for her, always will be hers, now can I have it?"

She received his news silently. Ripping the bracelet from her wrist, she handed it across.

Amos flew. To the end of the room, to the end of the hall, now dashaway, dashaway, dashaway all. To Ninth. Down. To Forty-seventh. Across. To Eighth. Tiring. Down. Past the drunks and the prosties, across Forty-sixth, Forty-fifth, past the tourists and the porno shops, threading his way through the thickening masses as he approached Forty-third and beyond, to Forty-tooth itself, where all the rotters, yahoos and errants of this world held their nightly jamboree, and just shy of Forty-two near the west corner Amos saw a pawnshop and as he knocked on the locked door the man inside gave the umpire's 'safe' signal, only here it meant 'shut' and Amos pounded on the door but the signal came again with more vehemence— only that wasn't the place—no—the guy on the phone was below, between Forty-first and -second, so he crossed Forty-two, still holding to the west side, checking every store front until he moved in front of it, as big as life, shy of Forty-first and open. Amos took a deep breath, started in, got a quick glance of his blood-smeared trench coat, took it off fast, casually flipping it over an arm lining side out. The Scotch was beginning to make itself known, so after he entered, Amos took particular time before he spoke, making sure all the words worked properly. "Couldn't have gotten here faster by whirlybird," he began, giving it the smile.

The young pawnbroker smiled back at him. He had

been talking to an equally young policeman but they stopped when Amos approached.

Amos wasn't too wild about the blue boy, since crazy Lila probably had an all-points spread on him by now, but that was out of his hands, no way to worry about that logically, there were enough problems he belonged to to keep him busy on that score. "I think I talked to you on the phone about two secs ago. About the watch? The one I told you about. From Rome."

"Oh you're the fellow."

"I'm the fellow." Amos hadn't expected the broker to be such a kid. At the least, Rod Steiger, but this one couldn't have been twenty-five yet. Probably the son. A family business. The cop wandered away and sat in a chair. Negotiations began. "I've never done this before," Amos said.

"Sure."

"Does everybody start off that way? You don't believe me."

The kid broker smiled. "I don't and they do."

Amos put the bracelet on the counter, the watch beside it.

"Pretty," the broker said, holding the bracelet to the light. "That's antique gold."

Amos nodded.

Reluctantly almost, the broker set the bracelet down, began to study the chronometer. "Keeps perfect time I suppose?"

"Perfect," Amos answered. "No, Not quite. It tends every so often to be a speck fast. I'm talking about maybe a couple minutes over a week, but that's the truth."

"Bought it in Rome you said?"

Amos nodded.

The broker pushed the top button, started the

sweep-second stop device. He pushed the bottom button, stopped it, pushed it again, sent the second hand
jumping back to the number twelve. "Let me take
these to the back and look at them, all right?"

"Be my guest," Amos said, and the pawnbroker
smiled again. He was a shortish kid, with blond hair
and he wore an Ivy League-type tweed sport coat, a
button-down white shirt, a rep tie. A Yalee, Amos
decided, as he examined the store. The policeman sat
idly in the chair. Chubby cheeks he had. The rest of
him was athletic enough, but the face was the kind
you tweaked in grammar school. Amos judged him a
very bored rookie, not the brightest either, as he sat,
surrounded on all sides by cameras and guitars and
transistors and Sony sets and two portable electric
typewriters placed very close together in one glass
counter, clearly the intellectuals of the establishment.

The Yalee came back. "What kind of numbers did
you have in mind?"

"I dunno," Amos said. "I really haven't done this
kind of thing before."

The kid put the watch on the counter. "I'll make
it fifty."

Seventy-five was what he'd paid for the damn thing
back in Rome, and besides that, watches were a lot
less expensive there than here. But fifty plus what he
already had made the Miami trip a certainty, and the
money for the bracelet would be icing on the cake.
"How much for the bracelet?" Amos asked.

"Fifty for both," the Yalee replied.

"You've got to be kidding."

"If my pop was here he'd give you less, I mean it.
You're lucky it's me, I really think that bracelet's a
beauty."

"It ought to be—you know what it set me back?—

you know what it costs to have a bracelet like that?—"

"Fifty's the top."

"—eleven hundred plus tax."

"Sorry," the Yalee said. "But I've got to close now so make up your mind."

"High pressuring doesn't work with me," Amos told him.

"I'm not high pressuring, but we've got to close by six and that's what it is now. So take the fifty or try for more in the morning. As my father would say," and here he went into a heavy European accent, " 'You vant? You don't vant? Eeder way I'm still breatink.' " He smiled again at Amos.

"I really do need more."

The Yalee shook his young head.

Amos hesitated.

And now the Yalee was looking at him funny.

"Just jack it up to seventy-five, could you do that?"

"Hey," the broker said then, "aren't you the guy? Sure you are, you're the guy, the song writer, I've seen your picture, what's your name now, I read all about you in *Variety*."

Amos decided it really was true, everybody did want to be in show business, and he also decided it was best to go unrecognized now, in case Lila had called the cops on him. "No, sorry."

"They fired you off *Annie's Day*—I saw that show, it stunk, they were crazy to get rid of you—"

"—thanks for the kind words but—"

"—*Francie* just happens to be, along with *Guys and Dolls* and *Carousel*, one of my three favorite musicals."

At least he was smart, Amos thought gratefully—he could have said *Sound of Music* and *Mame*.

"McCracken! You're McCracken the song writer,

am I right? I am right, I know I am. What the hell are you doing in a pawnshop, Mr. McCracken? *Francie's* still as big a hit as ever."

Amos shrugged. "I needed some quick cash and the banks were closed—it all came up very sudden."

"How much?"

"Five hundred wouldn't hurt—listen, the bracelet's worth twice that and I'll pick it up before you know it anyway, so you can't lose, honest."

"Hot *damn*," the Yalee said. "This really is fantastic." He gave Amos some forms. "Just fill these out, please." Amos nodded. "I write songs myself," the guy went on. "Not like you, but I've got a couple I'm not ashamed of."

Amos nodded, thinking here it comes.

"If you ever had a spare minute, it would really be an honor if I could play them for you."

"My pleasure," Amos said, guessing that it was time now for the honest-criticism bit.

"I'd really like to know what you think of them. You're a pro, Mr. McCracken, and there's no point to my beating my brains out if I haven't got it, so any honest advice coming from you, well . . ." He let the words hang.

Amos looked at the kid and if the best of his stuff made 'Trees' sound like a masterpiece, he'd still work with him personally, and if there was the least note of talent, he'd take the kid to his own music publisher and get him started, because to hell with being honest, there weren't that many times when people did you favors and you got a shot at trading back. "Nothing but honest advice," Amos pledged. "Word of honor." He finished with the forms, shoved them across the counter, took the ticket stubs the guy gave him and then waited while the five hundred was counted into his hand.

Grateful, Amos thanked and fled, but slowly, so as not to give anyone ideas. He left the store and started up to the crowd on Eighth and Forty-second and was making up his mind about staying on Eighth or cutting over when what he was afraid of sounded behind him. "Mr. McCracken, sir," somebody said, and before he turned Amos knew it had to be the kid cop, Chubbycheeks.

It was. "Guilty." Amos raised his right hand.

Chubbycheeks came up and stopped, fiddling nervously with his night stick. "I'm really sorry about this, I'm new and that's why I can't take the responsibility of letting it pass, but we got word within the hour about someone named McCracken."

"So?"

The guy was terribly embarrassed. "I hate to say this even but would you come with me to the station?"

Amos exploded. "Well Jesus, what the hell for?"

"I'm not sure, but a lady called up—something about a little girl."

You see any little girls lurking around me?

"No, but—"

"You got any idea how many McCrackens are in the phone book?"

"All I know is Frankie back in the place was all excited about how he's gonna play some songs for you, he said, and did I know who you were and I said how would I know and he told me and it rang kind of a bell, so would you come along?"

Amos stared bewildered at Chubbycheeks. "Tell you what. I'm meeting some friends for dinner—Sardi's—you call if you want to, check out my reservations—" He held his hands out in front of him, wrists together. "You can handcuff me and lead me away and I won't complain but first why not make certain which Public Enemy you're supposed to bring in."

"I have to obey orders, Mr. McCracken."

"Sure you do," Amos said soothingly. "God forbid you should be the first cop in Manhattan history to go against orders. All I'm asking is you see just exactly what your orders are." There were a number of locals gathered around them now, and Chubbycheeks' embarrassment swelled clearly with the throng. Doing his best to work on it, Amos practically shouted, *"Why can't you cops ever be reasonable?"*

"—Mr. McCracken, please—"

"—*all you guys understand is fight, hit, bang the public around*—"

"—if you could just lower the level, Mr. Mc-Cracken, we could talk about this—"

"—you gonna club me now?" Amos turned to the crowd. "Everybody stick around, he's gonna club me."

Chubbycheeks took Amos lightly by the arm, started to lead him across Eighth Avenue, leaving the people behind. When they got to the downtown east-side corner, they moved into the shadow of the bank where Chubbycheeks said, "You know I'm not gonna club you, I never clubbed anybody, you shouldn't have said a thing like that, I don't have to be this nice, Mr. McCracken, except Frankie said who you were, I could just drag you in, I've got the law if you want to think about it that way."

"Look," Amos said. "You're doing this nutty thing all on account of a last name."

"I think it was your first name too. I understand your being such a big deal and all, but if you're such a big deal and all, what were you doing pawning stuff?"

"Look—I'll go with you but I'll tell you this now—

when we get to the goddam precinct house I'm going to be very put out and false arrest is false arrest—so like the man said, let's reason together; you come with me to Sardi's, check out that I'm meeting these movie guys for dinner, that it's all set and above-board, and that way I won't be late and you can call in and get your facts and if it's me, I'll come happily, but how can I have some funny business going on with some little girl if I'm spending the night in goddam Sardi's, answer me that?"

Chubbycheeks hesitated.

"Look—we're on Forty-second, Sardi's is just up on Forty-fourth—how much can it set you back?—if you'd just walked up there with me when I first suggested it, we'd have the whole thing straight by now."

"You make sense, but—"

"—then just do what I say, huh? I'll buy you a beer after it's all straight."

"I don't drink on duty, ever."

"All right, I *won't* buy you a beer, but what the hell are we getting accomplished this way, now come on, walk me up there."

Chubbycheeks hesitated again. "You might try something funny."

"I'll walk with both my hands high in the air," Amos promised.

"—a thing like that on my record, a guy escaping me my first week in action."

"I'm a song writer, not Willie Sutton—"

"Better safe than sorry," Chubbycheeks said. He reached for Amos' arm again.

"I'll have your ass in a sling, you know that—"

Chubbycheeks nodded. "I got to take that chance."

Amos ripped his arm free. "I got friends," he said, too loud.

"Come on, Mr. McCracken, and no more bullshitting around." He grabbed Amos by the arm, roughly now, and started to shove him out of the shadows.

Amos sagged. "It's me you want." He leaned against the bank building, let it hold him. "I'm the right guy, but you got to not do it."

Chubbycheeks had his night stick ready now.

"Oh Jesus, please, I'm not trying anything, I'm just asking you one time to look the other way, you got any kids? Well I got one and that's all—I don't mean that's the only kid, I mean *all*, you get me, and if you only had one thing left to you and somebody was trying to take it away—*please*—see, I didn't do anything wrong, I had my eyes closed on the swing— all I did was shut my eyes—but she shouldn't take the kid away because of a thing like that, you understand, don't you, even if you got no kids, you got to understand."

"You're not making sense to me, Mr. McCracken. Now come on."

"No," Amos heard himself say.

Chubbycheeks looked at him.

"I won't go with you. I can't do that."

"I'm armed, and I'm a very good shot, now quit the crapping around—" Chubbycheeks began, ready for a lot of things but not for Amos' sudden screaming, *"Help—help me—he's killing me—HELP—"* and a dozen people froze on his words and Chubbycheeks glanced at them with "Keep right on going" but Amos moved on the glance, pushing off with everything he had, driving his shoulder against Chubbycheeks' shoulder, and as the boy in blue started to spin from the sudden charge Amos lit out for the corner and then he veered right, into the lights of Forty-second Street, because there was safety—in numbers if he could just use it right, if he could just be smart and not fuck up again the way he had been lately and as he made his quick way an exit door for one of the movie houses opened and two perfumed men stood there, lighting cigarettes before leaving, and Amos slipped between them and as the door closed, the darkness had him and he was thank you God in the clear, until he began having a lunatic fantasy with a humpback usher rolling up to him and calling for the cops and then Chubbycheeks came and like that it was all over, his final burst for freedom and to beat the fantasy Amos moved to the first door he came to and opened it and followed the stairs and ahead of him were cubicles for hiding and he slammed into one, sliding the lock across, safe.

Safe?

I am hiding, Amos realized, I am hiding in a toilet. I am hiding in a toilet in a men's room. I am hiding in a toilet in a men's room in a Forty-second Street movie theatre. And then another fantasy attacked him. Not that he got caught but that he *didn't* get caught. No one ever found him. And he had to live the rest of his life in a men's room in the basement in a Forty-second Street movie theatre. With nothing for sale but pocket combs and prophylactics. And nothing for intellectual stimulation but hot and cold running faggots and old men with weak bladders and pushers and users and an occasional conventioneer for comic relief and foul graffiti for wall decoration and the combined odors of pee, vomit and stool titilating the old nostrils.

This is *safe?*

Jesus, man, at least don't live in the toilet! Amos slid the lock open, stepped out of the cubicle into the room itself. It was empty for the moment, and the wall phone didn't look busted and with his last dime he dialed, Betsy coming in loud and clear on the first ring. "Amos?"

"Guilty," Amos answered, wondering how he could apologize, make it up to her, because he had never acted so cruelly to anyone as he had when he got her to give up the bracelet and she was such a sweet broad, that was really her sum-up, a sweet broad who didn't harm things and he had to make her know it wasn't him that hurt her, not Amos, not the standard one anyway. For he had been living in the crunch and he wasn't used to being there, and when you were in it, when you were trapped there you did what you had to do, and he was in it still, vised.

"Why aren't you back?"

"Well that's a very sensible question and the answer is, you remember that little sort of stew I told you I was in, well, the flame's a wee bit higher now, it's really bubbling and I'll get there when I can, how's the kid?"

"You better get back here—"

"—what do you mean?—"

"—just . . ." There was a pause. "Hold on."

Amos pressed the receiver hard against his ear, for in the background now his daughter was growing audible and then Betsy was saying, "Amos?" loud, as if he were just for chrissakes across the room or something and could bound right over and Jessica was worse now, he could hear her pain and sweet Jesus but she must have been hurting because she'd been a trooper through the whole fucking mess, no whining, no blubbering, tears only when the fear had her entirely, but now she was hitting all the high notes and now Betsy's feet were running toward the phone.

"Amos, she's starting to bleed."

Amos shook his head. "Not with that pressure bandage, Betsy—Doctor Contreras said—"

"—it's seeping out—"

"—it can't be, now listen, Doctor Contreras said it was fine, and the odds against anything happ—" But Betsy was gone from the phone now, running toward the pain, doing what she could to soothe, then back.

"Amos, what would it look like if she were starting to hemorrhage?"

"—no way—"

"—I think it's happening—"

"—Jesus—"

"—what'll I do?—"

"—keep her quiet—tell her, I don't know, but whatever she's going through, act like it's supposed to happen, like it's expected—I'm coming—tell her that, I'm on my way and it's gonna be fine." He slammed the phone, hit the stairs, flung a hand out, whipped the door back, stepped out into the rear of the theatre and if Chubbycheeks had been a quarter turn to the left, they would have been facing each other, but Amos grabbed the break and, since the cop was standing with an usher by the exit, Amos pivoted smartly toward the audience, marched down, took a center-aisle seat near the front. There, he spread his trench coat across as much of himself as he could without drawing attention, snuck a look around. Two seats to his right, a fat lady stared at the screen. Across the aisle, an old bum slept. And now, from behind him, he caught a glimpse of Chubbycheeks and the usher moving in among the seats, the usher starting to toss his flashlight beam along the rows.

Amos stared dead ahead and was confronted by Clark Gable in living color trying to find Susan Hayward. Gable was oldish kind of, too weary for his role, but he still had style and Chubbycheeks and the usher were moving very slowly down, still many rows

behind him. What do I do? Amos thought. I got a
little time to make a plan, but what the hell's a plan?

His first notion was just to casually saunter down
the front and take the first exit he came to, kind of
slip away, and that seemed logical until a guy got up
on the far side of the theatre and before he was even
on his feet the beam from the flashlight was full on
the guy's face, the usher clearly a goddam deadeye
when it came to accuracy with his weapon, a John
Wesley Hardin with an Eveready. So nobody was
going to edge out of the place unseen. So there went
plan A.

Gable was fighting now, but clearly a winner even
though the enemy had size and youth. Gable worked
inside the other guy's reach, tore his guts up with a
left, crashed him a right to the mush and it was over.
I saw this picture, Amos remembered. It was a best
seller, I think, what the hell's the name of it, the
background's the Orient and Clark baby was a soldier
of fortune and Susan was what, she was an American
but why was she visiting Hong Kong and what exactly was her occupation, think now think—

—*your baby's hemorrhaging, you son of a bitch,
get your mind off the movie!*—

Plan B. I need plan B. I got to just walk out of here
and my only break is time but time's only good if you
use it so use it, figure out plan B. Amos glanced
around, saw the usher's light, moving up a row closer,
coming to rest on each lost face, moving on. Silently,
Chubbycheeks moved alongside the flashlight man,
ready.

Amos turned front again, staring at Gable and a
great plan B, he fantasized, would have been maybe
a stink bomb, yeah, he had a stink bomb and he
lobbed it across to the far aisle and when it started
spreading the usher would head over there, Chubby-

cheeks with him, and in the commotion, whammo, he
was up and out and gone and back to Forty-eighth
Street and probably Betsy had the kid healed by now,
hadn't Betsy once said something about wanting to
be a nurse when she was a kid? Sure she had, that's
right, so maybe she'd taken enough nursing courses
to be able to fix the kid up, because it wasn't a hemorrhage, no, it was just a smear maybe, a little nothing
and Betsy had only called it a hemorrhage on the
phone because she was panicked that maybe she'd
forgotten too much of her nursing to bring it all under
control and maybe, maybe . . .

Chubbycheeks was coming closer now, the usher
moving inexorably on, brightening the faces briefly
with his deadly beam.

I got no stink bomb, I got no plan, not B or C or
any other letter. I'm in the crunch and I don't know
what to do because I'm just a feepy bastard who talks
a good game but folds inside the five-yard line—No!
Amos decided. I will not fold. I will find a plan.
Because I have to.

On the screen, Gable was talking to an untrust-
worthy-looking Oriental man. The Oriental raised his
inscrutable eyes, looked up at Gable, nodded, and in
the next cut Gable was driving his car along a Hong
Kong road and the fat woman next to Amos said,
"You tell 'em, you been to college!" very loud and
very clear.

Amos glanced at her. Her eyes were glued on Gable
as she said, "That's right, you tell 'em, you been to
college!"

From a few rows back, a male voice said, "Close
your hole, huh, lady?"

But the fat woman continued to stare at the screen
and Amos realized she hadn't heard the request from
the rear, she was a nut, a charter member of the

Forty-second Street Association, and she was off on
a wave length of her own.

"You're so goddam smart," the fat woman said, as
Gable continued his lonely drive, "you just tell 'em,
tell 'em all you want, they pay to hear you tell 'em,
you been to college!"

From another corner of the arena, another male
voice: "Shut your face or I'll have you thrown the
hell outta here."

Completely unaware, the woman watched Gable
drive. "Why the hell shouldn't they listen to you, you
been to college."

Amos was about to scrunch down deeper into his
seat when, from directly across the aisle, the old bum
was awake. Gable had transferred onto a motor
launch now, and as he roared off, the bum said, "You
don't expect me to believe that I hope," to no one in
particular.

It's another one, Amos realized, seeing the blank
look on the old bum's face. Gable opened the throttle
on the motor launch full, and the motor sound built
in the theatre.

"You sit there and you expect me to believe that?"
the bum went on. "Don't you have any respect for me
at all? You must really think I'm some kind of dumb
you expect me to believe that."

"Shut those two up!" several voices hollered.

Then a new voice, prissy, the usher's. "Here now,"
he said.

"You college boys sure know the answers," the fat
lady said.

The old bum said, "You never cared for me—you
cared for me, you'd never expect me to believe something like that—"

"Call the usher!" a new voice cried.

"Here now," again, prissy.

"And I thought you cared," the old bum said to Gable, who was running now, up along a hill toward a distant deserted tower.

The fat lady looked across Amos to the bum. "Shut your fucking face," she said to him, then turned back to the screen.

The bum looked across Amos to the fat lady. "Too ugly to hustle in the daylight, whore?" he asked.

Omigod, Amos realized—they're on each other's wave lengths, great.

"*Usher*," the fat woman called, "this drunk is pissing on your seats."

"Now I warned you, I warned you all," the prissy voice came, and Amos realized that it wasn't so great, the battle of the nuts, because the usher was coming toward him now and that meant there was no time left, no plan B to pull him out and as Chubbycheeks cried "*That's him!*" Amos involuntarily winced, waiting the force from the flashlight beam.

Which never came. In the darkness, Amos dared to turn in time to see the cop moving roughly across a row toward a trench-coated figure and the usher was supplying light and Amos took off then, because all the time he hadn't needed a plan, no, he was never any whiz at derring-do, what he'd needed was a break and this was it and when you got it, when you had Chubbycheeks triumphant over the wrong man, you didn't wait around, you went, so Amos did, to the front of the theatre where Gable loomed gigantic and dotted and left from there to the exit sign and then with some power Amos forced the door open and then he was on Forty-second Street and free and careful not to make a spectacle, careful not to bolt, Amos walked his legs off to the corner and across. He kept on heading west toward Ninth Avenue away from all the sound and all the people and as the lights from the frail carnival behind him dimmed, he began to run.

Not all-out. He had neither the speed nor the condition for that. Instead he forced his legs into a steady trot, covering the block in good time, not stopping once until he was all the way to the corner of Forty-second and Ninth, when he paused, panting, allowing himself the luxury to turn.

Chubbycheeks was behind him.

Not close. Still more than halfway down the long block but in the instant Amos watched he knew the other man had speed from the way his body covered the dark ground, and Amos fled against the light up Ninth, and Forty-third was easy, Forty-fourth too, and it was twenty short up and down blocks to the mile in Manhattan, so he should have been able to go one helluva ways full, but by Forty-fifth his legs had already turned traitor and as he moved the bouncing of his trench coat flung across his shoulders began almost to be heavy, so he was about to dump the damn thing when he remembered the big school between Forty-sixth and Forty-seventh just off Ninth Avenue and if he could make it there, if he could keep going long enough to make it there—Amos glanced back and his lead was over half gone, but worse, the other man was not slowing down and that didn't seem right, it didn't seem just or fair or any other goddam thing but there wasn't time to bitch about it, so Amos blanked his mind and cut across to the other side of Ninth and the sight of Forty-sixth forced him on and when he made it he cut left, into the darkness and as he passed the open schoolyard that went through to Forty-seventh, he did not stop but instead ran a dozen steps on, dropped the blood-stained trench coat to the sidewalk, then retraced the dozen steps, diving almost into the dark playground,

moving silently across it to Forty-seventh, hoping that
the law was tired enough to buy his feeble gambit
and think that Amos was still fleeing west along
Forty-sixth Street. When he got to Forty-seventh,
Amos wanted to stop, to listen and see if he was
safe but he knew that was madness because eventually, even if he fell for the coat bit, Chubbycheeks
was going to realize he'd been had and backtrack
and the logical place would be the schoolyard, and if
he waited to hear, Amos would have blown any advantage he'd made for himself, so he fought the urge
to rest, headed east to Ninth Avenue, then, stumbling
as best he could, he saw Forty-eighth Street slowly
coming to meet him. Drenched, pained, Amos turned
the corner toward Betsy's and he'd had it. He could
not run. No more. He moved as best he could, grabbing all the air his lungs could suffer, a genuine stab
of white coming straight in behind his eyes, all of
which made him slow to realize that Chubbycheeks
had not been remotely fooled and was, as Amos made
his erratic way, across the street in darkness, tracking
his feeble moves.

He could not believe that he had lost. After all the
madness, all the veering out of orbit he had done
this day, the final fact of defeat was simply unendurable. He had tried so hard, made every move, and
it didn't matter a damn, since there he was across in
the darkness of Forty-eighth, the victor, a kid cop, a
fat-faced, decent enough but brainless, frightened
boy. Amos made the jump to fantasy with no sweat,
and maybe it wasn't Chubbycheeks but just some
other lawman who wasn't looking for him at all, no,
maybe it was Chubbycheeks but he had realized in
the course of their travail how important having the
wee one was in Amos' lexicon and he had changed
his mind and decided to help Amos make Miami, no,

maybe . . . maybe . . . "Nuts," Amos muttered and he sank down. There was a pile of rubble by Betsy's and he rested on it, stones and parts of brick, and Amos laid his head on his weary arms, pondering his chances, because 'nuts' was what little boys said and his mother never let him catch or bat or play ball but she never minded his throwing things, since there was no way to damage those fingers doing that, so he threw. He made up games, and the enemy was most often the Yankees and it was always the last of the ninth, seventh game of the series and he was tired, he'd pitched and won three games already, but now in the final inning they were threatening, and the bases were loaded and two were out and there he stood, Joe D., and the manager asked could he do it, fire the old apple one more time and he'd nod and take the mound without warm-up and a tree would make as good a home plate as any and the count would go to three and two and then, the final rock in his hand, he would stand and face the enemy and fire, and across the street now Chubbycheeks said, "You done?"

"Right."

"Where's the little girl?"

"Inside." Amos gestured to Betsy's. "Hemorrhaging maybe."

"What have you got in your hands?"

"Nothing."

The law began advancing then. "Let's go."

Amos nodded, pushing himself wearily to his feet, started to Betsy's building, reached it, stopped.

The blue uniform was almost to the sidewalk.

Amos went into his sidearm move and the guy yelled, "Watch it!" but it was a good rock, it felt good when it left his hand, better when it hit, above the

eyes, and the law cried out, a shade of blood cur-
taining down across the chubby face, and Amos
pounded on Betsy's door and it opened with a buzz
and he was almost through it when he turned one
final time, caught the glint of metal, screamed "*All I
did was shut my eyes!*" before the sound came, much
louder than he ever imagined, and the velocity was
terrible too, driving him back through the tiny foyer
and beyond, but the pain was nothing beyond a
growing numbness emanating from his center, and
Betsy must have heard that noise too because her
door was open and Christ she looked so funny, deaf-
ened and numb and he saw the kid the second he
made it inside the room and what he'd fantasized
about Betsy stopping it, that was funny seeing the
poor child now, because the pressure bandage hadn't
held, the whole side of her face was blue and swelling like dough with blood bursting through the
stitches and Amos fell beside her and brought her
into his arms, their bloods mixing for the last and
only time.

Betsy looked down at them, waiting for Amos to
say something.

Holding his daughter in his arms, Amos muttered,
"Fifty was all the guy would spring for." He tossed
his trench coat over one arm. "Any trouble here?"

Betsy shook her head. "Asleep the whole time."

Amos got up, cradled the kid. "Thanks for sitting."

Betsy said nothing.

Amos moved to the front door.

"I hope you don't make it," Betsy said then.

"Oh I'll make it."

"I hope they catch you."

"That wouldn't be a good thing," Amos told her.

"What do you mean?"

"Nothing," Amos said, shrugging. His fantasies had been growing in violence all the day, but probably that wasn't cause for worry.

vi

The night air set her blinking.

"You're really turning into the lazybones," Amos said, carefully walking Forty-eighth Street.

". . . I just get . . . sleepy . . ."

"Listen, you get old, you get sleepy."

". . . I'm not old . . . you're teasing me again . . . you think it's easy to fool me but . . . it isn't, I really do know, where are we going?"

Her subject shift was occasioned by Amos' trying to hail a cab on the corner of Ninth Avenue. He pressed her to him with one arm, signaled with the other, but nothing stopped. "We're just following Doctor Contreras' orders, as you well know, since you were right there when she gave them."

"I didn't hear of any orders, what orders?" She was talking fast now, staring at him in the darkness. "What did she say, I really do want to know, I'm ever so anxious, Daddy, please tell."

"Well, as long as you're ever so anxious, I'll go over it one more time. Doctor Contreras said the best thing for your cheek would be some nice warm sunshine and I said fat chance in New York in the middle of February and she said that if I wasn't such a big deal, if I really cared for you getting the best treatment I'd take you bang down to Miami and plop you by some pool and let you bake and I told her I never said I was any big deal and she said, then do it, so we are. Doctor's orders." He shifted his baggage gently to the other arm.

During the shift, the kid winced.

"Sorry," Amos said.

"Sometimes it just hurts." She closed her eyes, beginning to drift again. ". . . when it's bouncy . . ."

And then she was out.

It happened so fast, the fastest yet, and what did that mean? By street light, Amos examined the child. She looked like chalk.

"Taxi!" he screamed. "Godammit, *CAB*," and he moved out into Ninth Avenue, waving his free hand. A couple of cars swerved by him, shouting, but who cared about them, screw them, because suddenly, down the block and slowing, came a Checker. "Airport," Amos said to the black driver. Doing his best to be gentle, he got in, spread the kid along the back. He took a jump seat and leaned toward her, holding her in place with both hands.

"Which airport?" the driver asked.

Amos hesitated only a moment before saying "La Guardia" because it was closest and all the airlines flew to Miami practically all the time, if you paid attention to the ads. He got off the jump seat now and knelt on the taxi floor, looking down at the kid's face, trying to spot improvement, anything rather than the steady paling that seemed to be draining her.

"What time you take off?" the driver said then.

Amos whirled on him with "Never mind what time we take off and don't bother asking where we're going, your job is to get us there so get us there!"

The black guy red-eyed Amos through the rearview mirror. Then he jammed on the gas, the car spurted forward.

Amos lost his balance in the move, clutched at the jump seat, finally righted himself. He was about to blast off when the black guy beat him to it: "Just gettin' you there."

Amos nodded, telling himself he didn't really need

any racial tension to top off the day. And he had to watch that paranoia, be done with it right now before it got him in trouble, because what the driver was probably saying wasn't 'What time you take off?' but 'How much time do I have to get you there?' and Amos should have answered that question instead. But he didn't. The guy had him pegged permanently as a George Wallace man, and nothing was about to change that, which was too bad because the guy was a cinch to remember him when the cops came asking questions. Obviously, they'd check all airport calls, and the black wasn't about to forget him now.

As the cab continued its move toward La Guardia, Amos stayed kneeling on the floor, holding the kid in place, every so often bending down very close, examining the bandage, anxious for any sight of blood. There was none. The stitches were holding, and that was good but Christ she looked pale, and that wasn't. But hell, the light stank and more than that, nobody looked human in February, not in New York City they didn't, and besides, once he hit Florida, she'd brighten up fast.

Amos continued his vigil, but his mind was on Miami. Since Sweet Betsy had gone pious on him, he'd never have a really big clump of cash, and that meant he'd have to use his credit cards. Lila could easily check that, so she'd know it was Miami.

Only it wouldn't be. Because they'd hit the road, him and the kid, staying nights where one of his credit cards could handle things, and so what if she was able to trace them, that wouldn't do her a damn bit of good because you could only really catch somebody if you had a notion as to where they were heading and that was the one thing he didn't have, any destination that might trap him. He'd just keep on the move, zigzagging through the south till Lila got panicked and then he'd make a deal with her, sure, but from strength, and he'd have it all written out by lawyers so she couldn't try to double-cross him.

That wouldn't be as good for the kid probably, all the driving around, not compared with life poolside, but maybe not all that bad either. Not if you had a convertible and kept the top down so she'd catch the sun and you stopped early enough in the afternoon for a decent swim and then an early supper and right to bed, no TV, nothing like that, unless the Flintstones were on at the right time. He'd let her watch the Flintstones and maybe Misteroger's and Captain Kangaroo in the mornings. Start the day with a good breakfast and the Captain and then cruise around the south with the top down and then a hot lunch and then a little more touristing and then a clean place for the night, let her practice her swimming, an hour on the boob tube, dinner and to bed.

Probably he'd go bughouse on a routine like that, but my God, the cause was worth it. He could never leave her alone, not with Lila on the trail. Most likely he'd read, maybe those Russian novels he'd missed along the way, improve his mind while the kid improved her body and they'd both come home the better for the jaunt. Cash might be a little problem but his American Express card was good for fifty in bills, a couple hundred if he'd settle for traveler's checks and they'd get by. Keep moving, use the noodle, change direction, shift around, waiting till Lila caved, then make like MacArthur, return in triumph.

"You goin' to Boston?" the black said, as they roared along the La Guardia approach.

Amos checked himself. "Just get us to La Guardia, okay?"

"I got to know if you're goin' to Boston."

"You don't have to know—"

"... Miami ..." very soft.

"I'll handle this if you don't mind," Amos told her.

"... but you said Miami was where—"

"The whole world doesn't have to have its nose in our business, all right?"

"—but Daddy—"

"—*don't talk back to your father!*" He almost never yelled at her like that, but then she almost never did anything that ticked him off, and even then he usually phonied his way out of the situation, lied to her, like he'd lied when she'd sung 'Once in Love with Amos' at his eighth-anniversary party, and the cab was filled with clapping people and his daughter was running first to Lila, and Amos was filled with damaging power. And maybe it all dated from there, from the kid going first to the mother, all the troubles he'd come heir to, all the watersheds he'd crossed. Except that was too easy an explanation, his whole life fragmenting just because he was afraid Lila had edged him out forever in the wee one's world.

"Listen, mister, there's no point in our going at each other, but the Boston shuttle, see, it's off by itself; the other airlines are all in one building but I guess you want National if you're going to Miami."

"We're not actually stopping there," Amos said. "We're just changing planes and flying to the Caribbean." He leaned down close to the kid. "Daddy just teases everybody," he said.

"... when's Mommy coming ...?"

"Soon," Amos said. "Just as soon as is humanly possible." He stopped. "Actually Mommy's very busy these days—Mommy's got lots of little odds and ends to do these days, with neat guys like Frederick A. Hunter and she may not get around to letting us bask in her warm presence for quite some little time. The thing of it is, Mommy's not making this trip, that's what I'm trying to tell you."

The cab turned into the arrivals ramp. Amos paid, gathered up the kid, got out. "Have a good time in Miami," the black said to Jessica.

"The Caribbean you mean," Amos reminded.

The black looked at him funny.

Amos lugged the kid into the airport proper. Dead ahead was a lit statue of Fiorello himself and to the right and left were stores: book, toy, drug, gift. The up escalator led to the Observation Deck, the down to the airlines offices. Amos was very much aware that two pseudo-businessmen types supposedly lounging in black leather chairs were watching him too closely, so he grabbed the down escalator to the airlines offices. The wall clock said twenty of eight and the schedule behind the ticket sellers had the next flight to Miami set for eight-thirty and you couldn't fall into it much better than that. Amos propped the kid in a corner of the airlines office, went up to one of the selling ladies.

"Yes, sir?" the girl said.

But she wasn't looking at him, Amos realized. Oh, she pretended to be, she made out like he was the center of the world, but who she was looking at was another guy down the counter and who he was looking at was the kid.

"Yes, sir?" the girl came again.

"What's all the big thing?" Amos wanted to know. "You were looking at him and he was looking at God knows what, let me in on it."

She smiled. "I'm sorry, sir," she said. "Office joke."

Amos studied her. "Two for the Miami flight, coach, one grownup, one kid."

The girl got out some forms. "Is that a son or a daughter?"

Amos studied her again. "I don't see how that's so relevant, do you? You always go around asking people if it's a boy or a girl and like that?"

"Yes, sir."

"Oh," Amos said. Then, quickly, "How much will it come to, one way? My name's Hunter, Fred Hunter, and my daughter's named Betsy, now do you want credit card, traveler's checks, what?"

"Either will be fine, Mr. Hunter."

Amos nodded, had his wallet half out before he realized how close he'd come to blowing it all; he was dead right to use the phony name, no point in practically begging Lila to start right off checking Florida, but once the airlines people saw they had a guy going under an alias they'd have the cops on him fast. So what he had to do was pay cash, only he didn't have enough, which meant he'd have to change his traveler's check, but he couldn't do it here. "Be right back," he told the girl, hurrying to Jessica, carrying her to the escalator, taking it up to where there were stores and he could make his financial transaction without suspicion.

The kid was slumping badly again, her eyes half up into her head and she'd never seemed paler. Amos jiggled her a little. "Hey," he said, "we're going to the toy store to get you some goodies, so tell me what you want?" Not that he expected her to be capable of speech, but she looked so weak now that he wanted to make sure she was still sort of okay. He bounced her again in his arms, her eyes almost opened, and he entered the toy store. "Wow what a terrific selection."

She began to close her eyes.

A saleslady came up and very loudly, to his daughter, Amos said, "Next time you take a nap in the afternoon when I tell you to." He smiled at the sales-

174 WILLIAM GOLDMAN

lady. "She was just so excited about flying I couldn't get her down."

"Once they take it in their heads not to nap, there's nothing you can do," the saleslady said. She had a round face, pretty for fifty, pretty always, probably, but no ring on her left hand. And she would not stop staring at Jessica.

"We're looking for a sort of junior stewardess bag."

"We have a lovely selection," the saleslady said, leading Amos toward a rack of plastic bags, but staring all the time at Jessica.

"You haven't got one that says 'New Orleans'?"

"No, sir."

"Which'll it be, babe?" Amos jiggled the kid again. No reaction.

Amos grinned. "Out like a light, just like a woman, we'll take that one," and he pointed to a blue job. "And maybe some crayons too."

The saleslady took the items to the cash register. Amos got out his traveler's check and signed. "Sir . . .?" the saleslady began, and she could not take her eyes from the child but Amos put an end to that quick enough, starting very loud into "Now you'll probably want identification so here's American Express, Diners,' Carte Blanche," and he flipped the cards toward the pretty woman. She gathered them up, started to study them, then went back to looking at the kid. "Listen, we're in something of a hurry if you don't mind."

"I'm sorry, but your child—"

"—the name's McCracken, Amos McCracken if you can't read my writing," Amos said, confident that the minute the name was truly spoken he could find a fantasy somewhere, and then the airline ticket lady from downstairs was pointing at him and then the two pseudo-businessmen types who had tried not

staring when he first entered the airport lounge
grabbed him and they ripped the kid from his arms
and Amos tried crying out "Easy with her" but they
wouldn't obey, he was too tired to fight them, too
tired even for a decent fantasy since the saleslady
was done checking his credit cards and was pushing
them back to him along with the cash left from his
purchases and the kid was growing heavy in his arms
now as he tried shifting her around so he could grab
the cards and the forty-odd in change and stuff them
back into his pockets. The saleslady was staring at the
kid again and Amos threw a strange city at her, anything to get her off the kid: "I just hope we don't miss
that Atlanta plane."

The saleslady started to say something, stopped,
blinked, "I thought you said you wanted a New Orleans bag."

"That doesn't mean I have to go to New Orleans,
does it? I can ask for any bag I want to, it's not
against the law. Are there statutes on the books
against asking for New Orleans bags 'cause if there
are, I'd sure like to know about 'em," and he began
losing control now, the look on the saleslady's face
rocking him, and the kid was strangely heavy so he
had to hurry on. Louder: "I can ask for a New Orleans bag or an Atlantic bag or a Henry Aaron bag
or a Willie Mays bag or a Mets bag or a Jets bag
and," he kept on, his voice weird and it scared him,
everything scared him suddenly as the pretty saleslady's face drained into fright and he was back at the
playground with the drunk coming round the fence
crying "Here!—Here!" in horror at what he saw
that Amos couldn't and now the pretty saleslady
could see the kid's face and Amos couldn't and she
started whispering, "Sir—sir—there's something very
wrong—"

"—there isn't—"

"—there's something wrong with your child—"

"—she had an accident, a little accident, gimme those things—" and he reached for the blue bag and the crayons.

"—let me call the airport doctor—"

"—she's seen a doctor—"

"—please—I'm afraid—her head—the angle of her head—"

"—I know all about it—"

"—there's something terribly wrong with the angle of her head, let me please call . . ."

Jessica pitched forward toward the counter.

Amos caught her. His right hand stopped her body. But her arms flopped bonelessly on. And her neck was limp. Her head dangling. And there was no life left inside.

Amos folded.

He crashed to the floor, the child cradled in his arms. The bloody deed was done and there he was, surrounded by toys, staring at the maimed rag doll he had formed from his child.

Oh dear God, dear God, this isn't what I meant when I got up this morning . . . this isn't how I planned to end the day. . . .

There were very strong tides swelling up inside and for a moment he tried to brake them. But they rolled right on. His grief broke like a thunderclap. All the hurts that had been building funneled from his throat, and seated midst the trifles of childhood Amos could only turn his weeping face away as the saleslady knelt by him. "It's all right, you mustn't feel ashamed, it's only the brave men who cry," she said, and then she said, "Thanks for coming, come again," and Amos assured her of his undying patronage as he scooted down the mall to the drugstore,

where he bought a comb, toothbrush, a small tooth-
paste, enough, he figured, to see the kid through the
first Miami night. He jiggled her a little. "Anything
else strike your fancy?" She managed to shake her
head, so he paid, had everything tucked into the blue
stewardess bag, and then zipped back down to the
ticket offices. It was five to eight when he paid in
cash and the uniformed girl behind the counter
flashed a "Thank you, Mr. Hunter, have a good trip
now," to him and he gave her his best grin in return,
went back to the kid, who was propped in a chair in
the corner of the room, close to half awake.

"We board in fifteen minutes," Amos said, tucking
the tickets into his inside suit-coat pocket. "Any last
requests?"

She indicated none.

"Hey I'd bet you'd be a little more comfy all
stretched out, huh," and he picked her up, carried her
to the downstairs lounge by the escalators.   There
were a series of square black leather-covered otto-
mans placed along a white tile wall. Amos laid the
kid out full, saw to her comfort, then seated himself
by her head. Directly in front of them were perhaps
a dozen large green potted plants, and beyond the
plants, outside, a round lit fountain sent water splash-
ing. "Hey," Amos shook the kid's shoulder. "Take a
peek—that's a preview: all that water, all that green;
just add a little sunshine and you've got where we're
going. It's gonna be so great, maybe we'll try surfing
once you get your strength back up to snuff."

She stared at the green plants, at the fountain. ". . .
Daddy . . .?" she said then.

"What?"

". . . Daddy . . ."

"Right here."

There was a long pause before she said, "I want to see Pierre."

"Huh?"

". . . I want to see Pierre . . ."

"Someday, honey."

". . . I want to see him now . . ."

"Well he's not around, so you're doomed to disappointment."

"I really do want to see him . . ."

"He's not here, didn't you listen?"

". . . he might be . . ."

"Excellent logic, he certainly might be. He might not be too."

". . . you could look for him . . ."

"I am, baby, see? I'm just squinting all around but he's not here, so rest easy, they're gonna call our plane soon."

". . . it's just very important, Daddy . . ."

"Change the record, why don't you?"

". . . please, I do so need to talk to him . . ."

"It drives me right up the pole when you whine, now knock it off."

". . . I do . . ."

"Oh for chrissakes," Amos said, standing up, looking into the ticket-selling area. "He's not there, he's not around, now are you satisfied or do you want me to search the whole airport?"

". . . please . . ."

"Well I'm not going to leave you alone here, you're six." He sat down again.

". . . I'll be good . . ."

Amos began playing a few tunes on his kneecaps.

". . . I will, I'll be so good . . ."

"Like now, you mean? Good like now?"

". . . I just do have to see him . . ." and she shook her head to one side. The move caused her pain but she shook her head again, to the other side, harder, and the pain was worse, but that didn't stop her from shaking her head back and forth, and she was really starting to hurt herself now. Amos didn't know what she was working herself into, her head twisting from side to side, her battered face contorted. "You're so stubborn, you really are the most stubborn child, I could blister your bottom for you except you know I won't because you're so under the weather and you're taking advantage of my good nature and you know it and don't think I'm going to forget this, now quit moving your head and close your eyes, get some rest, I'll look around upstairs but if you make any more trouble this trip there's gonna be *consequences*," and she closed her eyes tight, lying immobile, nothing moving at all until the words *"Sacre nom de Dieu"* came some time later and then she saw a mustached man storming past, wearing a white shirt, the sleeves rolled all the way up.

". . . Pierre . . .?"

The mustached man continued on by.

". . . Pierre . . .?"

He stopped, looked back, hesitated, then moved over her, staring down. "Not for you," he said finally, shaking his head.

". . . what . . .?"

"Tell your make-up man that Pierre say that next time to either put ze beauty marks on both cheeks or do not put zem on at all."

". . . it's a bandage, it isn't any beauty thing . . . it's a real bandage . . . I didn't look in the playground . . . I just caused so much trouble, Pierre . . ."

"Who have not cause ze trouble? *Le premier* meal I make for the English queen I forget to light ze oven and ze hard sauce come out soft."

". . . Pierre . . ."

"I have no time for you now, Small."

". . . but I'm going to Miami with my daddy, Pierre . . ."

"*Bon*. I have a cousin who make the *salade* at Le Fountainbleau. When you dine at Le Fountainbleau you will of course say hello to my cousin. But never eat the *salade*. *Au 'voir*, Small."

". . . take me home, Pierre . . ."

"Huh?"

". . . please . . . I really do need to go home . . . I don't want to go to Miami . . . I don't want to go anywhere . . . not with my daddy . . . I don't want to be with my daddy . . . he's gone all scary and I just do want to go home . . ."

Pierre folded.

". . . Pierre . . .?"

Pierre didn't say much.

". . . are you all right . . .? have I hurt your touches or anything . . .?"

Pierre smiled. "I am sad for Amos only, Small. I have hear much of what you say about him—very little escapes us in the food industry. I fret for my friend, *naturellement*, but I have *pas de* sadness for myself: tonight is my greatest triumph, Small. True. All the chefs come from all the world to do me honor. They have rent the famous Grande Ballroom of La Guardia Airport. So tonight, in return, I unveil my *spécialité*."

". . . steak-chop . . .?"

"*Non*, more better even than that." He lifted her up. "Come. I take you home but I cannot cook for you *ce soir*—perhaps I sing you to sleep instead, have you ever hear me do this?"

". . . no . . ."

"Madame De Gaulle says I am without equal.

Whenever Charles have *le insom* and cannot sleep, I sing him there. Do you know 'Frère Jacques'?"

She nodded.

"I write that for my brother Jimmy." He took her up the escalator toward the observation walk. "I want to be sure all my friends are landing as they should. If they were late, the *spécialité* would be ruined."

". . . what is it . . .?"

He dropped a dime into the observation-deck turnstile, shouldered his way out onto the walk that curved around to where the taxis were. "Wing of pork."

The night was growing cold now, the heat of the day done.

". . . pigs don't have wings. Pierre . . ."

"They do now that I cross them with the turkey. This is not an easy venture, Small; it take me years."

". . . to make them the same size . . ."

"*Non*—the problem here was getting them to like each other—look—" He pointed out toward a silver jet taxiing toward them. "*Bonsoir, mes amis*," he cried aloud. "They are from France, Small. And those—" He shouted "*Achtung!*" to a dark plane starting to unload luggage. "Germans," he explained. He gestured toward the entire giant plain. "Look, Small—every flying machine you see comes filled to do me honor."

". . . all of them . . .?"

"*Oui.*"

". . . oh Pierre, you really are the greatest cook in all the world . . ."

"*Cook!* On this night, the small one chooses to insult me—"

". . . chef, I meant . . ."

"*Bon.*" He continued walking slowly toward the taxis. "It's really very strange, is it not?"

"... what ...?"

"Well, you are getting what you want: to go home. And the great party all for me; who would not want a thing like that? Yet neither of us smiles, I wonder why."

"... I don't know, Pierre ..."

"I don't know too." He shook his head. "There must be many unanswered questions about us both."

ABOUT THE AUTHOR

WILLIAM GOLDMAN was born in Chicago in 1931 and now lives in New York with his wife and two daughters. After graduation from Oberlin College, he earned his M.A. at Columbia and turned to writing. He has been considerably acclaimed for his work, which includes novels, a mystery, plays, screenplays, and a controversial critique of Broadway, *The Season. Butch Cassidy and the Sundance Kid,* an original screenplay, brought Mr. Goldman an Academy Award. His novels are *The Temple of Gold; Your Turn to Curtsy My Turn to Bow; Soldier in the Rain; Boys and Girls Together; The Thing of It Is . . . ; No Way to Treat a Lady* and *Father's Day.*

RELAX!
SIT DOWN
and Catch Up On Your Reading!

- [ ] THE LOVE MACHINE by Jacqueline Susann. (T5400—$1.50)
- [ ] AIRPORT by Arthur Hailey. (T3982—$1.50)
- [ ] PORTNOY'S COMPLAINT by Philip Roth. (T4899—$1.50)
- [ ] MYRA BRECKENRIDGE by Gore Vidal. (T5730—$1.50)
- [ ] THE GANG THAT COULDN'T SHOOT STRAIGHT by Jimmy Breslin. (Q5740—$1.25)
- [ ] TRAVELS WITH MY AUNT by Graham Greene. (T5786—$1.50)
- [ ] THE HARRAD EXPERIMENT by Robert Rimmer. (Q4690—$1.25)
- [ ] CHARITY GIRL by Georgette Heyer. (N6727—95¢)
- [ ] SIDDHARTHA by Hermann Hesse. (Q6909—$1.25)
- [ ] ONE DAY IN THE LIFE OF IVAN DENISOVICH by Alexander Solzhenitsyn. (N4639—95¢)
- [ ] THAT MAN CARTWRIGHT by Ann Fairbairn. (T6935—$1.50)
- [ ] HER by Anonymous (T6669—$1.50)
- [ ] PRINCIPATO by Tom McHale. (Q6695—$1.25)
- [ ] DIARY OF A MAD HOUSEWIFE by Sue Kaufman. (N3715—95¢)
- [ ] CALIFORNIA GENERATION by Jacqueline Briskin. (Q5834—$1.25)